For Alison
Merry Christmas '96
love
Uncle Bill

The
Dragon
in the Cliff

The
Dragon
in the Cliff

A NOVEL BASED ON THE LIFE OF
MARY ANNING

BY SHEILA COLE

DRAWINGS BY T. C. FARROW

LOTHROP, LEE & SHEPARD BOOKS   NEW YORK

First Edition 1 2 3 4 5 6 7 8 9 10

Library of Congress Cataloging in Publication Data
Cole, Sheila. The dragon in the cliff : a novel based on the life of Mary Anning by Sheila Cole ; illustrated by T.C. Farrow.
p.   cm. Summary: Recounts the girlhood of the woman who made many of the important fossil discoveries in the early nineteenth century, yet never received the credit she deserved. ISBN 0-688-101968
1. Anning, Mary, 1799-1847—Juvenile fiction. [1. Anning, Mary 1799-1847—Fiction. 2. Paleontology—England—Fiction. 3. Collectors and collecting—Fiction. 4. De La Beche, Henry T. (Henry Thomas), 1796-1985 —Fiction. 5. Women—England—19th Century—Fiction.] I. Farrow, T.C., ill. II Title PZ7.C67353Dr 1991 [Fic]—dc20 90-40455 CIP AC

TO MICHAEL,

who knows how to make dreams come true

CONTENTS

PREFACE

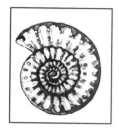Although *The Dragon in the Cliff* is a work of fiction, it is based on the fragmentary facts available about a real person and the place and time in which she lived. Mary Anning was, in fact, the first person to discover the fossil of an entire marine dinosaurlike creature. She made this discovery in 1812 when she was thirteen years old. At that time the sciences of geology and paleontology were in their infancies and the existence of dinosaurs was as yet unknown. Scientists were just beginning to accumulate evidence that species evolve, putting in jeopardy long-held beliefs about the special place that human beings occupy in the natural world.

Finding the remains of a giant dinosaurlike creature would be exciting under any circumstances. But finding them under the circumstances of Mary Anning's life is a drama of a very special kind. Mary Anning lived at a time when women were excluded from scientific activity even if they came from well-to-do families. The fact that Mary Anning was not only female, but that she came from a poor family in a small town and still managed to contribute to the scientific work of her time is what makes her achievements so remarkable. It was in trying to imagine what it must have been like for her to have made such a discovery and how it affected her life that I came to write this book.

Sheila Cole
Solana Beach, California
January 2, 1990

The
Dragon
in the Cliff

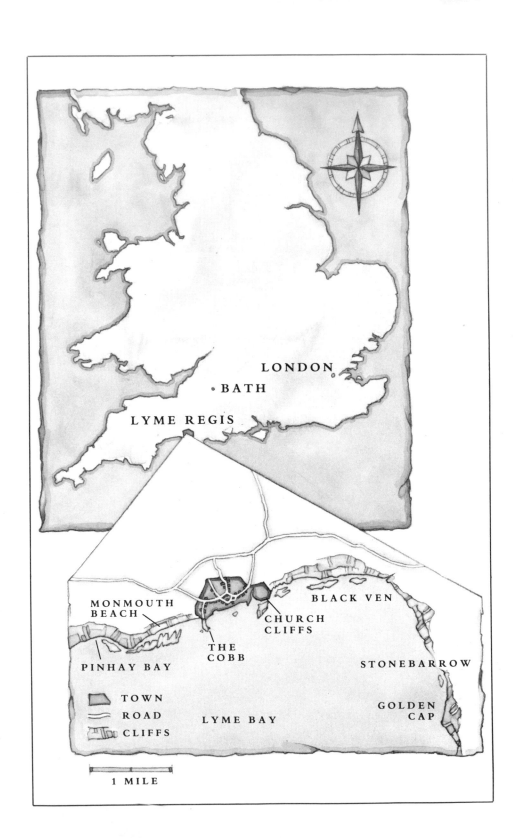

LONDON

BATH

LYME REGIS

MONMOUTH
BEACH

BLACK VEN

CHURCH
CLIFFS

THE
COBB

PINHAY BAY

STONEBARROW

TOWN
ROAD
CLIFFS

GOLDEN
CAP

LYME BAY

1 MILE

I AM LOST

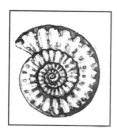Outside my shop everything is quiet. All of Lyme, from the high to the low, are in their beds. All except me, and I cannot sleep. My brain is feverish from thinking about what has happened and what I should do. There is no one I can talk to about this, not even Mama. No one would understand, not my old friends, certainly, and not the geological gentlemen who are my patrons. I am alone, cut off from everyone, different from everyone, belonging nowhere. I am lost except for the fossils. To others they are only cold stones, the petrified remains of animals long dead, but to me they are so much more—my livelihood—but even more than that, my passion and the reason for everything—my difference, my isolation, and my joy. Would I be like the other girls in Lyme if I gave up fossils? Could I give them up? I don't even know. I am lost. Perhaps if I begin at the beginning I will understand how I came to be caught between two worlds and know better what I should do.

HOW I STARTED

There are people in Lyme who say that it isn't the fossils that made me different from others, but the lightning. On the nineteenth of August, in the year 1800, when I was fifteen months old, there was awful thunder and terrible lightning that made all of Lyme wonder.

The way it is told, a company of horsemen came to give a riding exhibition in a field near town. Elizabeth Haskings, who was watching after me, took me there so that she could see the jumping. A thunderstorm broke out not long after the crowd assembled and everyone scattered. With me in her arms, Elizabeth ran for shelter under a large elm. Fannie Fowler and Martha Drower also took shelter under the tree. There was a bolt of lightning and a terrible clap of thunder, the loudest ever heard. After a minute, a man saw the group lying motionless under the tree and called the alarm. Upon arriving at the elm, they found the girls dead.

I appeared to be dead as well. I was taken from Elizabeth Haskings's arms and carried to my parents' home. My parents were told to put me in warm water and by so doing revived me. People say that from that

day on I was livelier and brighter than others in Lyme.
That is why they credit the lightning for my being
different and being able to discover the stone monster.
They even say that is why I am able to talk to the
cleverest scientists in England, though I am only a girl
and am uneducated.

I don't think it was the lightning that set me on a
different path. I believe it all began with Papa and his
"curiosities." That is what people in Lyme call fossils.
Papa would go down to the beach to collect them every
spare moment he had. Mama did not approve. "It's
foolishness," she would say. "A waste of time. You are
a cabinetmaker, Richard."

Papa would answer Mama patiently, "Molly, we
have been at war with Napoleon for years now and
there's a blockade which is ruining better men than I.
I don't have many new orders for furniture these days
and those old stones, as you call them, bring in money."

Papa's answer would quiet Mama for a while, for she
knew as well as he that travelers on the coach from Bath
and visitors who came to bathe in the sea and stroll
along the shore stopped at the little table outside the
cabinet shop to buy Papa's curiosities.

Papa started to take Joseph to the beach with him
when Joseph was nine years old. Of course, I wanted to
go, too. I wanted to do whatever my brother did. "It
isn't fair," I would protest. "Why can Joseph go and not
me? I'm almost as big as he is." Standing on the tips of

my toes, I would add, "Bigger than John and Ann. They're just babies, and I'm going to be seven."

"We're not going to the beach to play, Mary. I'm teaching Joseph so that he can help me," Papa would say, putting an end to my pleading until the next time.

One day I was not to be put off as easily as usual. I pulled at Papa's arm as he put on the old coat he wore to go collecting and begged to be taken along, promising, "I'll help. I'll be good."

Mama pulled me from him roughly, saying "Enough! Mary, you can help me here. There is no water for washing up. Go fetch some and be quick about it."

I took the yoke with the buckets, but instead of going to the pump, I followed Papa and Joseph up the Butter Market and down Long Entry, past the baths, keeping a safe distance behind them for fear of angering Papa. Oh, how I wanted to go curiosity hunting! Though, the truth is, I had little idea of what that meant. It was enough for me that Papa liked to do it and that he always came home with his face aglow from the sun and the wind and with exciting new curiosities to show us. Now Joseph was going, but not me. I watched jealously as the two figures, one tall and thin with a gray sack slung over his back, and one smaller with a blue cap, made their way down the steep path to the beach below. Then I turned back toward the pump. After filling the buckets, I struggled home under their weight.

The morning dragged on forever while I did my chores. I braided rushes for a new rug, listening all the while for the door of the shop downstairs to open. As soon as I heard it, I dropped the rushes and ran downstairs to the shop calling, "Let me see what you found. Let me see." I pulled the curiosity basket from Joseph's hand and immediately started to empty it. "Did you find this?" I asked, holding up a sea lily, with its delicate branches and flowers.

"Papa found that one. I found this one," he said. His long, oval face was unusually serious and important as he showed me a bullet-shaped curiosity. "Papa says it's called a thunderbolt."

"Is it really a thunderbolt, from the sky? Tell me, Papa!"

"No, my dear," Papa replied, "it only looks like a thunderbolt. It's a curiosity."

"Was it a living creature once?"

"They say it was."

"What kind of creature?"

"I don't know, my little monkey. No living creature I know of looks like that."

"Where did you find this one?" I asked, holding up another curiosity.

In the midst of my questions I was called away to watch the little ones while Mama set out the soup and bread for dinner. But as soon as I could, I stole downstairs to the cabinet shop again where Papa was at work on the lathe. I picked the fossils up one by one. "Papa," I shouted over the noise of the lathe, "Where did you find this one?"

Seeing that I was trying to say something, Papa removed his foot from the pedal so that he could hear me. I repeated my question, he started the lathe up again, shouting the answer as he turned the wooden block on the machine.

With all the shouting, it didn't take long before Mama called me away again. When I came upstairs, she glowered at me. "Your Papa is working and you are stopping him with foolish questions. What a bothersome child! I can't understand what has gotten into you."

Though usually I was sensitive to a scolding, Mama's cross words that day had little effect. I was determined to learn everything that Joseph knew about curiosities and to be useful to Papa, too. That afternoon I went down to the shop again to sit at Papa's side while he cleaned the new finds. "Can I do one?" I asked.

"You must have a light, sure hand or you'll break the curiosity. Sit here and watch. You can brush away the bits and pieces of mud and shale I pry off with my needle," Papa said.

I picked up the brush and watched as Papa worked the needle, carefully lifting the softer stone from the harder curiosity. "Papa, do you think someday I'll be a help?" Papa continued prying away the softer stone.

"You are a help now, Mary. You run errands and you don't forget. You do your chores, you help Mama with the little ones, and soon you will learn to make lace. Mama depends upon you," he said without looking up.

I cocked my head and brought it low so that it was on a level with his. "Papa, that's not what I mean. I mean a help to *you* with the curiosities. Helping Mama with the chores is dull."

He put down the needle, stood up, and patted my head. "Dull or not, they must be done, Mary. We all have dull things to do." He went over to the box on the floor where he kept his finds and began to search through it.

"But hunting for curiosities isn't dull. It's like a game," I said after a minute.

Papa looked up from the box. His pale blue eyes took me in appraisingly. A smile slowly spread across his face, but he did not answer.

I remember my first fossil-hunting expedition as if it were yesterday. One day not long after I started to help Papa prepare the curiosities, when I was pleading as usual to be allowed to go to the beach with Papa and Joseph, Papa suddenly turned to Mama and asked, "Molly, don't you think we might let her come along?"

"Richard, whatever are you thinking?" Mama replied. "Girls don't belong down on the beach."

"Only this once, Molly. When she sees how dirty

and rough it is, she won't want to come again. She'll be happy to stay home with her knitting and the little ones."

"I need her to keep them from getting underfoot so I can get my own work done," Mama objected.

"Just this once," Papa said.

I was in my cloak and wooden clogs and out the door before Mama had a chance to protest. I was going to find something magnificent and prove to Mama and Papa that I should be allowed to go curiosity hunting!

It was early. The town and the surrounding hills were shrouded in wet, gray mist, closing us into the small world of the shore. We walked along, glad to be out in the sharp salt air with the sound of the waves in our ears.

No sooner did we approach the cliffs of Black Ven than Papa began our lesson. "Joseph, where is the tide?" he asked.

"It's going out, Papa," Joseph replied, glancing over his shoulder at me with a self-satisfied look.

"Yes, and that is the time to go curiosity hunting, when the tide is going out. Then you have plenty of time to do your work. You must always keep an eye on the tide and be sure to leave the beach in plenty of time before it is high again."

"Papa, you once forgot," I reminded him.

"Yes, and I'm thankful that I'm here to tell the tale. I was hammering right over there on a rock to break out a curiosity, when suddenly I realized that the sea was lapping at my feet. The beach on either side of me was underwater and in a short time I would have been underwater, too, if I hadn't climbed the cliff."

Joseph and I looked up at the wall of Lias cliffs with their layer upon layer of rock and dirt. It seemed impossible to us that anyone could climb to the top. Only an occasional bush or tuft of grass softened their almost perpendicular ascent from the beach. I squeezed Papa's hand, glad that he had escaped and certain that I would never, never forget about the tide.

We walked on to the far end of Black Ven. "We'll work the slide today," Papa said, pointing at a dark mound located at the foot of the cliff. "It's in slides like that one that I often find the best curiosities. It's easier than trying to get curiosities out of the cliff. That's hard work and it is dangerous. But if you have the patience to wait and let storms break down the edges of the cliff, then half your work is done for you."

The slide, which hadn't looked very big from a distance, turned out to be a mound taller than Papa and several yards wide. What looked like dirt was actually a mixture of limestone, shale, clay, and dirt.

Papa and Joseph put down the tool bags and the curiosity basket, and I suddenly realized that I didn't have any tools. "What shall I do?" I asked Papa. "I have no hammer or chisel."

"There are many curiosities to be found in a slide like

this that are already free. If you find one that needs breaking out of the rock, we'll help you."

I looked carefully at the slide, picking up bits and pieces of limestone and shale, turning them over to see if they contained anything, and tossing them aside, trying to find something that would impress Joseph and Papa.

The first one to find something was Papa, who called us over to look at a golden-colored stone disc with a pattern like a tightly coiled rope.

"It's a golden snail," Joseph said.

"It's not gold and it's not a snail," Papa corrected him. "It's an ammonite and it's only fool's gold. See, it's not yellow like gold, but a brassy color. It should fetch a pretty penny. People like ammonites and this is a nice-sized one."

"How did the curiosity become yellow like that?" I asked Papa as he wrapped the ammonite in rags that he had brought from home.

"I'm not certain, my dear. Somehow the metal must have replaced the ammonite's hard shell. But how, I do not know."

Now I wanted to find a fool's gold ammonite, too. But the first thing I found was not golden at all. It was a gray stone disc bigger than the palm of my hand, hollowed out in the middle with a ridge protruding from one side.

Joseph glanced over at it. "A verteberrie. Throw it away, Mary."

I thought he was just being spiteful. I made a face at him and took the curiosity to Papa, who was splitting a piece of rock open with his hammer and chisel.

"Oh, that's a nice one," Papa said. "Too bad the travelers don't buy them." Seeing how disappointed I was, he added, "But the collectors are always interested in them. Perhaps Miss Philpot will want it for her collection. Wrap it up well so it doesn't break and put it in the basket, Mary."

"What is it, Papa?" I asked.

"Part of the backbone of an animal."

"What kind of an animal?"

"No one knows, my dear, but from the looks of it, it must have been a big one, a very big one, I'd say."

"Has anyone ever found all the parts to a creature like that?"

"No, but if you keep looking, perhaps you will."

Joseph called to us excitedly. He had found something. He climbed down the slide and handed me an irregular slab of gray rock to look at. On the rock, delicately outlined in reddish brown, was a small fish. Once it had been a fish that swam in the sea, but now it was a faint impression in a piece of rock. How strange! How wonderfully strange it was to hold a once-upon-a-time fish in your hand.

Joseph's brown eyes glowed with pride when he took the fish from me to show Papa. I went back to my hunting determined to find something valuable, too, anything that would convince Papa to let me come again. I looked at the dirt and rocks in front of me, searching for a sign, something that would tell me that a curiosity was there. I pulled the rocks out of the mound and looked at them with even more care than before to make certain that I missed nothing. But I only managed to find another thunderbolt before Papa called for us to stop. "The tide is well on its way in, children. See how high the water is on the Cobb," he said, pointing to the breakwater and harbor.

I was quiet as we walked back. "See here," Papa said, pointing to a section of the cliff. "That rock might give way if there is another storm. I tell you, that'll be a rich place to hunt. We should find some real beauties if we get down to the beach before the slide is washed away by the sea." I glanced at where he pointed and turned away. It really was no concern of mine. I hadn't been useful. I would have to stay home with Mama and the little ones.

"You did very well," Papa said, patting Joseph on the back. "It's a lucky day when you find a fish. Squire Henley will want to see it. It should go for a good price. You really are learning." Then, noticing my silence, and guessing at my unhappiness, he said, "Don't be discouraged, Mary. Maybe next time you'll find the entire beast and not just the verteberrie."

My heart leapt. Next time! He said I could come next time! I couldn't contain my happiness and raced ahead, scaring the sanderlings, who rose up with a shrill cry as I drew near. The sun broke through the morning fog, turning the sky a light blue, which the sea reflected in deeper shades. As if a curtain had been lifted, we could see the patchwork of green fields, edged with dark green hedgcrows that stretch up the hills above the rocky cliffs. To the west, the thatched and slate-roofed buildings of Lyme climbed up the sides of the steep valley from the bay and spread out across the hilltops.

That night, lying in bed beside Ann, I was too excited to sleep. I was going to find that giant creature whose verteberries I found in the slide. How proud Papa would be. Everyone would come from miles around to see it. Seeing how good a curiosity hunter I was, Mama would let me go to the beach any time I wanted to. In the midst of these thoughts, I heard my name in the whispered conversation that Mama and Papa were having in their bed across the room.

"Richard, you're fooling yourself if you think you put an end to Mary's pestering about the curiosities. Did you see how excited she was when she came in? Couldn't wait to show me what she had found. Ran upstairs with all that mud still on her. It was foolish to let her go. Now there will be no end to this curiosity business with her."

"Ah, there's no harm in it, Molly," Papa replied.

And if anything ever really has a single beginning or a single cause, that was the beginning of my fossil hunting and the different turn my life has taken.

CHAPEL SCHOOL

 Lizzie Adams, whom I used to consider my closest friend, now does not approve of me. She says I think that I am better than everyone in Lyme, that the fossils and my fame have made me proud and unyielding. She is by no means the only one of the people in this town who feels this way. From the beginning, there have been those who disapproved of my fossil hunting, who believed that it was not a proper pursuit for someone of my sex.

I had gone collecting with Papa only a few times before the Reverend Gleed's wife, a very large woman with powdery skin, a fleshy nose, and colorless, thin hair, called on Mama.

Mrs. Gleed came from Taunton to Lyme with her husband, the leader of the Dissenting congregation to which we and many other artisans' families in Lyme belong. Taunton being bigger and more prosperous than Lyme, which has fallen on hard times, Mrs. Gleed considered it her duty to enlighten us poor, backward souls. Hearing her in the hall downstairs, Mama, who was preparing dinner, quickly wiped her hands on her apron—which was none too clean—looked at her image in the glass, and straightened the cap on her honey-colored curls, all the while directing me. "Clear away the table. It is unsightly. Hurry, Mary. . . . Oh, John is crying. Pick him up and quiet him, please. Where is Ann? Is she into any mischief? Mrs. Gleed will be thirsty, she'll want some cider."

Mama took John from my arms, and before I could finish clearing the table, Mrs. Gleed was standing in the middle of the room. "Mrs. Gleed, how nice of you to call," Mama said pleasantly, greeting the reverend's wife, who was winded from climbing the stairs.

Mama offered her a chair, and Mrs. Gleed dropped into it with a sigh of relief. "My, my," she said, shaking her head, "What a climb."

Mama gave me a look, reminding me of the cider. On the way down the stairs to the scullery I heard Mrs. Gleed say, "Mrs. Anning, I don't know how you and Mr. Anning manage those stairs, they're so steep. I would call more often if it did not mean climbing up here to your little room."

I heard Mama laugh nervously. Her discomfort made me realize for the first time that to some people our living arrangements, which are much the same as everyone else's that we know—a small scullery behind the shop, a large room above the shop, and another small room under the eaves for sleeping—are poor.

I opened the door to the scullery, filled a glass with

cider from the jug, and brought it back upstairs, placing it on the table in front of Mrs. Gleed. She emptied the glass, wiped her lips with her handkerchief, and turned to ask me, "How old are you, Mary?"

"I am seven, ma'am," I answered with a curtsy.

"Old enough to attend school so that she can learn to read and write," Mrs. Gleed said to Mama.

"I already know how to read," I told her proudly. But I was speaking out of turn, and Mrs. Gleed paid no attention to me.

"I've been teaching her myself," Mama said.

"School attendance is daily. She will make more progress there."

"She is doing well here, Mrs. Gleed," Mama said quietly, holding firmly onto John, who was struggling to get out of her arms. "I've begun to teach her to make lace. She has a deft hand and learns quickly. She helps me with the little ones so that I can do my work."

I took John from her arms and put him on the floor where he could practice walking and I could watch him without being sent away.

"That may be, Mrs. Anning," Mrs. Gleed said, "but what I hear from others is that the child goes down to the beach to collect curiosities. It is even said that she sometimes goes there by herself."

Red blotches appeared on Mama's cheeks. "She does not go to the beach alone, only with Mr. Anning and her brother Joseph. And that is because she cries and begs until we let her go. She loves her brother and wishes to do whatever he does."

"Her will must be broken," Mrs. Gleed insisted. "And the school will do it if you are too fond to do it yourself. Spoiled children are ripe for the devil's harvesting."

Mama sighed, "I suppose you are right, Mrs. Gleed." She looked down at her hands. "It seemed no harm. She is but little still and she so wants to go. . . ." She stopped for a moment. Then in a low voice as if speaking to herself, she said, "Sometimes it seems a pity that she is a girl, she is so quick."

Mrs. Gleed's face did not soften. Rising from her chair, she replied, "Mrs. Harris will take care of that. She will teach her what is proper." At the door Mama said, "I must speak to Mr. Anning about it."

"If you explain it to him, Mr. Anning will see that it is for the girl's own good," Mrs. Gleed replied.

When Mama told Papa that people did not think it right that I went to the beach to hunt for curiosities, he replied scornfully, "There are always people who think they know how others should live, people who would hold everyone to their own narrow, ignorant ideas of what is proper. Let me see them live their own lives as they should, and then I will follow their good advice. The child is under my roof, and it is my duty to raise her as I think best. I see no harm in her gathering curiosities on the beach."

Mama met his icy blue glare with her own gentle gaze. "But the child must live among these people, Richard, and they talk and condemn her for it."

"Who are these people you speak of?" Papa asked angrily. "Ignorant old gossips who know nothing of science, care nothing for knowledge, and foolish young ones who follow them. Certainly Miss Philpot does not say anything against curiosity hunting, and she is respectable. I have seen her on the beach myself. I have even seen some of the London ladies venture out to hunt for curiosities."

"But Mary is not the daughter of a wealthy London merchant as is Miss Philpot, nor is she a London lady," Mama countered. "She is a cabinetmaker's daughter who lives here among people who disapprove."

The result of this discussion was a compromise: I was allowed to go curiosity hunting, but I was also enrolled in the chapel school, where Joseph was already a pupil in the boys' class. There, in that low building behind the chapel, I spent my days in a small, noisy room filled with girls, learning to read the Holy Scriptures, to write, sum, embroider, and knit. School was daily, except Sunday, when we went to chapel in the morning and again in the afternoon. The result was that only rarely did we have a chance to go the beach with Papa.

I went to school for almost three years, during which time every effort was made to break my will, as Mrs. Gleed predicted. I remember one such incident with pain to this day.

It happened soon after I started school. There was a storm that lasted for several days, soaking the town and the surrounding cliffs with rain and lashing the beach with ferocious tides. Except for our forays to school, where we arrived wet through to the skin, Joseph and I stayed at home. We grew increasingly irritable with each other as one rainy day followed another. The rain finally came to a stop on a Sunday, and though it is customary to do little that day but go to chapel and read the Bible, Papa, Joseph, and I were eager to get out of doors. "To stretch our legs," Papa said to Mama. "We'll return in time for the Reverend Gleed's sermon."

Being the Lord's day, we were not going to hunt for curiosities. We just wanted to see if there were any new slides. In our search for a slide, we wandered far to the other side of Black Ven and did not hear the bells for afternoon services. We did not realize how late it had become until we met Mr. Clerkenwell coming home from chapel. He saw us but, turning away, did not acknowledge our greeting.

"Mama will be angry," Joseph said.

Papa and I knew that he was right, and we also knew that there was nothing we could say to excuse ourselves. Missing chapel was an unpardonable sin for which we

were certain to be punished. The first punishment came
from Mama. We were not greeted when we arrived,
nor did Mama ask us what we had seen. We washed up
in silence. No one but Ann and John spoke, and even
they soon grew silent.

Joseph and I read our Bible lesson aloud under
Mama's disapproving gaze. The lesson was one I love,
the first chapter of the Book of Genesis telling how in
the beginning the earth was without form and darkness
was upon the face of the deep. And God said, "Let there
be light," and there was light. God separated the light
from the darkness and the light became day and the
darkness night. On the second day God created heaven;
on the third earth and the seas and all the plants of the
earth; on the fourth day the sun to rule the day and the
moon and stars to rule the night. On the fifth day God
created the great sea monsters and all the creatures of the
sea and the winged birds; and on the sixth day he created
man.

I had heard this passage any number of times, but
listening to Joseph read this time, my mind wandered
to the curiosities. If the curiosities were once living
creatures, as Papa said they were, then they must have
been created by God. Most of the curiosities we found
were like creatures that live in the sea. Were they the
creatures that God made on the fifth day? How did they
turn to stone? And how did they get from the sea into
the cliffs? I wanted to ask someone these questions, but

I knew not to ask Mama. She would have been shocked by such thoughts and would have given me a slap if I had dared to utter a word about them.

Instead it was she who was asking me questions. "What did God do on the seventh day?".

I stood and recited: "God blessed the seventh day and hallowed it, because on that day God rested from the work of creation."

"And what are we, his children, to do on the Sabbath day?" Mama asked Joseph pointedly.

"On the seventh day we are to rest from our labors and worship God and his creations," Joseph mumbled.

Mama turned to me. "Why?"

"Because it is God's commandment. And those who disobey his commandments are punished," I replied.

She nodded, satisfied that we had learned our lesson. She closed the Bible, but she did not relent in her punishment. We ate our bread in silence, and then went to bed without as much as a good night.

The second punishment came the next day. Knowing full well that I had yet to face Mrs. Harris's wrath, I took my time getting to school, going there in a round-about fashion to avoid meeting the other children from our quarter of town, and slipped into my seat between Emma Cruikshanks and Lizzie Adams only seconds before we were called to order.

"Where were you yesterday afternoon?" Emma wanted to know. "You're going to catch it from her."

Emma was always saying things like that with a certain amount of delight. She, of course, never did anything wrong herself.

When I told her that we were walking on the beach and didn't hear the church bells ring, her round blue eyes widened until they positively bulged. She shook her head and said, "Missing chapel and walking on the beach on the Sabbath! Mary, you'll get at least seven for that. She gave Ann Beer six for less."

Seeing my terror, Lizzie Adams tried to soothe me. "If you explain, maybe she won't. You did mean to come to chapel, you just didn't come in time," she whispered as Mrs. Harris entered. We all scrambled to our feet and stood stiffly at attention as she marched to the table that served as her desk. "Good morning, girls," she said in her singsong voice.

"Good morning, Mrs. Harris," we chorused.

" 'Tis payday," Mrs. Harris announced, opening the roll book on the table before her. She smoothed the pages with her fat white hand. "Adams," she called.

The penny stuck to my palm as I watched Lizzie Adams stride to the front of the room to pay for school. I prayed over and over to myself—Dear Lord, please let her get it over with quickly and I promise that I will never miss chapel again—knowing that my prayer would not be answered and that it did not deserve to be.

Susanne Allen's name was called. She hurried to the

front of the room, bent over and whispered something in Mrs. Harris's ear, and scurried back to her seat.

"She doesn't have a penny," Emma whispered. "Mrs. Clerkenwell says the Allens are to be turned out of their lodgings because they can't pay the landlord. They have applied to the parish for aid." Though normally I would have looked upon Susanne's position with a mixture of pity, fear, and horror, I was too afraid myself right then to give Susanne much thought.

"Anning," Mrs. Harris called.

I could feel everyone's eyes on me as I made my way to the front of the room. Avoiding meeting Mrs. Harris's eyes, I dropped my penny on her table and turned to go back to my place on the bench.

"I haven't finished with you, Mary," Mrs. Harris stopped me. "Please tell us why you did not attend chapel yesterday afternoon."

For a second I considered lying, telling her that I was not feeling well, but I knew that I would be quickly found out if I did, and then I would be in even more trouble. "I was out walking on the beach with my brother and father—" I was cut off by a titter of laughter.

Mrs. Harris's eyes imperiously swept around the classroom, silencing everyone. "Your father will have to answer his own conscience and will suffer God's judgment for his sin. But you followed him and you will have to answer for that, Mary."

"We meant to come, but we didn't hear the bells," I tried to explain.

"You didn't hear the bells," Mrs. Harris repeated, her voice growing louder with each word, her sagging cheeks quivering.

"No, Mrs. Harris," I answered.

Mrs. Harris pulled herself to her feet and leaned over the table toward me. "You went out on the beach on Sunday to look for curiosities."

"We didn't look for curiosities. We were taking a walk."

"You are telling a falsehood. You have broken the Lord's own commandment: On the seventh day you shall rest."

I tried to explain, but Mrs. Harris cut me off with an order to Emma to fetch the cane. Emma was, as usual, only too happy to be of use. I looked around the room. My eyes met Caroline Gleed's. She stared back at me coldly. Jane Lovett smiled. Lizzie's eyes were cast down.

"Hold your hands out and look at me," Mrs. Harris ordered. "Now repeat: I have offended the Lord by laboring on Sunday and shall be chastised," she said, bringing the stick down on my knuckles.

I drew back in pain.

"Don't move!" Mrs. Harris ordered. "Now again."

"I have offended the Lord by laboring on Sunday and shall be chastised," I repeated as the stick came down on the back of my hands again, again, again, again, and again, ten times in all.

"Any more absences from chapel and you will no longer be welcome here," Mrs. Harris said, dismissing me. Dazed with pain, I continued to stand there, holding my bleeding hands out in front of me. Lizzie whispered loudly, "Mary, put cold water on your hands." I turned and went to the cloakroom where there was a pail of water. I poured a little on my handkerchief and used it to wipe the blood off my hands. They stung as I touched them, and the pain brought tears to my eyes. I wrapped the handkerchief around one hand and then put both my hands under my arms and went back to my seat. Everyone except Lizzie turned their eyes away and drew their legs in to avoid me as I passed. She passed her handkerchief to me without a word, and I wrapped it around my other hand.

No doubt Mama noticed the swollen red welts and cuts on my hands at dinner that noon. Perhaps she thought it right that Mrs. Harris punished me for missing chapel. She didn't say a word about it and neither did I. The only one who mentioned it was Joseph. "I see that you got it, too," he said as we were walking back to school after dinner.

"Did you?" I asked.

He nodded and pointed to his backside. "Promise not to tell Papa. It'll upset him that we were punished because of him." I promised not to tell, although I would not have minded at all if Papa became angry and took us out of school.

That afternoon when Mrs. Harris was listening to the beginning readers, and I was sitting off to one side doing my sums on a slate, Jane Lovett came up to me. She bent over, bringing her face close to mine, and stared into my eyes without saying a word. I flinched. She moved closer so that our noses almost touched, and I could see the golden flecks in the blue-green irises of her cold, angry eyes and the white tips of her dark eyelashes. I looked away, but she grabbed my chin and turned my face back to hers and held me there in a viselike grip. My throat tightened. I could not breathe, but I did not know what to do. Then as suddenly as she had come, she turned and walked off. She came up to me the next morning as I was writing my spelling words on my slate. This time she held her stare for what seemed like forever. When I tried to turn away, she gripped my arm tightly and turned so I was still facing her. Tears came to my eyes. Her eyes glinted with satisfaction when she saw this. She let go and walked off.

For some days after this Jane kept springing out, catching me unaware at my lessons or my knitting, staring into my face until I flinched. Other times she stole up behind me and imitated my every move. I did not know she was there until I saw the other girls laughing. I whirled around to catch her, but she was too fast and I was afraid to chase her.

I became nervous and self-conscious trying to be on my guard against Jane. I did not sleep for several nights thinking about what I should do to stop her. I did not talk to Lizzie about it. She saw how Jane was tormenting me, but offered no help. When I became desperate, I considered telling Joseph about it, but I dismissed the idea. It was too embarrassing to talk about to anyone, even my own brother. Besides, I knew that he would tell me to hit Jane, and Jane was bigger than me.

Then one day she came up to me as I was leaving school. She poked her face into mine and said, so that everyone could hear, "You know what you are, Mary Anning? The Stone Girl. A curious curiosity." Without stopping to think, I reached up and slapped her cheek hard. Jane brought her hand to her face, which was reddening from my blow, and stepped back. All the other girls and boys who were pouring out of school onto Coombe Street stopped to watch. William Trowbridge called to Jane, "Hit the Stone Girl." But before she could, I walked away, using all of my self-control to keep from running. Someone else yelled "Stone Girl," after me, but I did not turn around to see who it was.

Lizzie caught up with me as I turned onto Bridge Street, not far from home. "I'm glad you finally did something about Jane," she said, falling into step with me. "She won't bother you again, I can tell you that. You really surprised her. But you know, Mary, if you weren't so proud, Jane would never have gone after you. You act as if you are better, and it makes the other girls angry."

"What should I do," I demanded, "cry for them when I was punished? Grovel for their pity? I tried to explain to Mrs. Harris what happened, but she wouldn't believe me. They don't care about me. They think I'm strange because of the curiosities. They were glad to see me punished."

"No, they were not glad, Mary. They would have listened to you, and they would have taken your side if you hadn't been so proud and unyielding and had gone to them and told them what happened."

"No, they wouldn't. They don't care. They are glad I was beaten, because they hate me," I said, breaking into tears. I ran into the house.

I was still afraid that Jane would continue to torment me in the same way, or worse, when I returned to school the next day, but she left me alone. She did not stare at me or imitate me again. Neither did any of the other girls. They might not have approved of me; they might have thought I was proud and unyielding, but they realized that I would not be bullied any longer.

THE TURNING POINT

 It was not what happened at school, however, that led to my present unhappy state, but the misfortunes of my family.

Papa had always talked of having a shop in which chairs, settees, and couches could be made from start to finish. To turn this dream into reality, he apprenticed Joseph to old Mr. Hale, the upholsterer on Coombe Street. As an apprentice, Joseph was (and still is) little better than Mr. Hale's servant. He goes to the pump for water, to the coal monger's for coal, sweeps the shop and the house as well, runs to the ironmonger's for nails, to the cloth merchant's for cloth and braid, picks up the furniture to be upholstered, and delivers it to its owners when the job is done. But all the while he is learning the different parts of the upholstery trade. Entire days pass by without our seeing him.

He stopped going curiosity hunting with us. When he asked permission to go along, Mr. Hale told him, "If your father had wanted you to be a curio man, he'd have kept you home. He sent you here to learn the upholstery trade and that's what you're doing." Joseph did not ask again. Still, from time to time, he steals down to the beach to see what he can find.

It was not long after Joseph went to live at Mr. Hale's that the spells of coughing and night sweats that Papa had been suffering from for years became more frequent and serious. He often had to stop what he was doing to rest for a while. Still, he would not call a doctor. "Quacks," he called them. "Doctors are only good to take your blood and your money, neither of which I can afford to part with," he would say, when Mama talked of calling in Dr. Carpenter. He believed that the best thing for a cough was the fresh sea air. But the fresh sea air did not cure Papa's cough. Neither did drinking sea water, as the fashionable visitors to town do. Finally, when Papa collapsed on the beach and had to be helped home by the cockle man, Mama overrode his objections and called in the doctor.

Dr. Carpenter told us that Papa's consumption was far gone. When the doctor left, Mama went back upstairs to where Papa was lying in bed. We could hear her weeping through the closed door. Hearing Mama cry, the little ones started to cry, too. John shrieked. I picked him up and tried to quiet him, jiggling him up and down in my arms. Ann stood at the foot of the stairs looking up at the closed door, bleating like a little lamb, "Mama, Mama." Tears were streaming down her red face. I slipped my arm around her shoulders, but she would not be comforted.

Papa recovered somewhat in a few weeks and returned to his work in the cabinet shop. He also insisted
on going to the beach to collect curiosities. Mama
pleaded with him not to go, but he would not listen.
"I'm still well enough to feed my family," he replied,
taking the sack of tools from the shelf. He went out the
door without looking back.

Mama was beside herself with worry about Papa's
health. Thinking that Papa might listen to his older
brother, Uncle Philip, she sent a message to Bridport.
Uncle Philip walked the ten miles to Lyme, arriving on
Sunday when Papa was out visiting friends.

"He's a stubborn man," Uncle Philip said to Mama.
"Never could tell him anything. If he's determined to
go down to the beach, he'll go no matter what you say.
Someone should go along with him."

Mama, who was sitting opposite him at the table,
threw out her hands helplessly. "Joseph cannot go. He's
bound to Mr. Hale, and John's still a baby. Mary is old
enough, and she's a strong lass, but she's in school most
of the time."

Uncle Philip took several deep puffs on his pipe,
sending clouds of blue-white smoke into the air. We
watched the smoke thin in the air for what seemed like
minutes. Then he said, "Molly, you know I don't agree
with your sending Mary to school. Girls don't need
book learning. Gives them ideas. A whistling woman
and a crowing hen are neither good to God nor men.

Let her go along to watch after her father."

"Oh, Mama, may I? May I?" I burst in.

Mama did not even turn to look at me. "He'll not complain about that," she said to Uncle Philip with a bitter laugh. "He's been taking her along since she was just a little one. Didn't care what I or anyone else said against it."

"Well then, all the better. She seems eager enough," he said, turning to me, "aren't you, Mary?" I nodded and he continued. "She can keep an eye on him while she helps with the collecting and brings some money in. I've none to spare, Molly. And Richard tells me there hasn't been much work in the shop."

Mama sighed. "I don't like it, Philip," she said. "It's not work for a lass. The neighbors talk. They blame me for her going down there where she doesn't belong. You know they are carrying on the free trade on the beach now with Napoleon and the blockade. It's not the smugglers themselves I worry about. They are our own folk. Some of our neighbors are in that line. It's the fights with the Customs men that scare me. She could be caught between the two."

"Like it or not, Molly, it is better than being so poor you cannot feed yourself. And Richard will never apply to the parish for relief. He's too proud to accept hand-outs," Uncle Philip replied.

Mama looked up from her work with tears in her eyes. She bit her lip and looked away without saying anything. And so it was decided that my schooling was to end.

It was as if I had been set free, free from Mrs. Harris and her beatings, free from the boredom of sitting with the other girls at school practicing fine needlework, free from their sharp tongues, their backbiting, and their snobbery. I would miss sitting near Lizzie Adams and whispering with her when Mrs. Harris's back was turned. But there was little else about school I would miss. I was going to the beach with Papa.

The next morning I rushed through the breakfast dishes and bounded into the shop to begin my *real* education. Seeing me, Papa shook his head. "Mary, you are sadly mistaken if you think that collecting curiosities is always exciting. Now that you are here with me every day you shall see that I have my share of slow, hard work, and today is one of those days. I have curiosities to prepare for the travelers, and that is just as slow and careful work as lace making or needle-work."

"Oh, but Papa, I love working down here with you," I protested.

"We'll see what you think after you have been at it a bit," Papa said dryly. "I'm going to teach you how to cut an ammonite so that its insides can be seen. The ladies who come to bathe in the sea find their swirling chambers beautiful, and I can sell all I can cut."

He showed me how to choose which curiosities to

open and how to saw the soft stone with a toothless metal band and wet sand. "The trick is to keep the sand in the path of the saw wet," he said, loosening the peg in the barrel he had rigged so that water dribbled onto the sand from a hole in the bottom. "Actually it is the wet sand that does the cutting, not the saw."

I was clumsy, and I found that while the stone was not hard as stone goes, it was hard enough to make my progress slow. Papa took over from me after a while so that the ammonite would be ready for the next day when the coach came bringing the travelers and visitors who were our most frequent customers. When the curiosity was finally cut through, Papa set me to polishing it with wet sand on a slab of limestone. For a final polishing he showed me how to use a wet leather cloth covered with chalk dust. "Now it will fetch a pretty penny," he said approvingly, when I showed him the polished fossil.

"It's so beautiful, and it took so long. Can't we keep it ourselves?" I begged.

Papa shook his head. "No, Mary, my dear. We can't keep it, lovely as it is, no more than Mama can keep the lace she makes, or I the tables and cabinets."

I was disappointed and asked, "Why is it only rich people who can have fine things?"

"You know as well as I, Mary, they have them because they can afford to pay for them," Papa replied. "And I don't need to tell you that we need the money

it will bring in. So we had better get on with the work and get some other things ready as well."

The next morning, before going off to the smith's to have the chisels sharpened, I set the ammonite out on the table with the other curiosities we had for sale. It was gone when I returned. I meant to ask Papa who bought it, but my question was forgotten in the rush of customers.

The days that followed were, like the first, filled with lessons—where to find curiosities, how to get them out of the rock, and how to prepare them so that they show to advantage. Papa showed me the best places to look for certain curiosities. I knew that the cliffs were made up of layers of rock, one laid upon the other. But it was Papa who told me that Lias means layers. "You'll find different curiosities in different layers. Some places, like the Black Ven marl and the Church Cliffs' blue Lias, are rich in curiosities, and others, like the upper green sand over toward Golden Cap, have little of worth."

The next few months were crammed with such lessons. Now I can see that Papa was in a hurry to teach me everything he knew. And I, not truly understanding why he was paying so much attention to me, was happy just to be with him and eager to learn everything he taught me.

October is often mild with blue skies and deceptively warm days that make one forget the cold, gray days that lie ahead. It was on one such fine October day, when he was feeling strong, that Papa set out for Captain

Locke's in Charmouth, just two miles away. He did not return when we expected him. It was already dark when Joseph stopped by to say hello. Mama, becoming anxious, asked Joseph to stay until Papa returned. She lit the candles. The little ones were hungry. Mama put supper on the table. We ate, listening for Papa's footsteps. Even John, who was only five years old, understood that something was the matter and was quiet. We finished supper and still Papa had not returned. We cleared the table, washed the dishes, sat, and waited.

There was an abrupt knocking at the door to the shop. We all jumped up at once. Papa would not knock. Who could it be? All of us tumbled down the stairs, one on the heels of the other. Joseph reached the door first and opened it. It was Mr. Clements, who worked for the Customs. Standing behind him was a large, red-bearded man we did not recognize, holding Papa in his arms.

"We were on the trail of some smugglers when we found him lying halfway down the cliff. He must have fallen," Mr. Clements told Mama, as Joseph and I took Papa from the arms of the red-bearded man.

I don't know how we got Papa up the steep, narrow stairs to bed, but we did. For several days he lay there, too weak to say anything. Then he seemed to be regaining his strength. The Reverend Gleed came and sat by Papa's bedside for some time. When he came down, he told us that Papa wanted to see us.

Joseph, who had not returned to Mr. Hale's since

Papa was brought home, was the first one up the stairs, followed by Mama, John, Ann, and me. Mama sat down next to Papa and grasped his limp hand in hers. John stood next to her, finger in his mouth, almost hidden by her skirts, and right behind him was Ann, wide-eyed with fear.

"Now, Molly, don't cry," Papa whispered, as Mama bent over him, smoothing his hair back. Tears slid down her cheeks. "Don't cry," he whispered hoarsely, struggling to sit up.

Mama tried to help him, while Joseph arranged the pillows behind his back to support him. I remember thinking as I watched them, how small he seemed. He had been a big man, and now he was small. Yet I could not remember him growing smaller. When he was sitting, Papa looked at us. He tried to say something and began to cough. Helplessly, we watched as each cough racked his body. When he stopped coughing, he fell back on the pillows weakly. Mama wiped the blood from his lips.

He looked out the window. Our eyes followed his gaze. "It's strange how you think that everything will stop when you stop," he said after a minute. "But see, the sun is still shining and the tide is coming in. They'll be here long after I'm gone. So will you, my dears, so will you. But I'm afraid to think of what will become of you. I've tried my best to provide for you, but I have failed."

"Now, Richard—" Mama started to protest.

But Papa cut her off, "These are hard times, Molly, no use denying. . . ." He turned to Joseph. "I planned for you to work here with me, son, but that shall not be. You'll be on your own when you finish at Mr. Hale's. You will be a fine upholsterer, that I know. And you will be a fine man, too. Be good to your mother, brother, and sisters. They need care and protection, and will only have you to look to." Joseph nodded, wiping away tears with the back of his hand.

"Mary, my child, you are a good girl, and you will be a fine woman. I have tried my best to prepare you for what is coming in the only way I know how—the curiosities. They are not enough, but they are something. Listen to your mother, she knows what is best. And to Joseph, who will be the man of the family. Help them." I was crying, and I could not manage to say anything. I threw my arms around Papa and clutched him tightly, as if holding him would keep him. Mama gently pulled me away.

I did not hear what Papa said to Ann. Mama held John up for Papa to kiss, then she motioned for us all to leave so she could be alone with him for a few minutes before he fell back asleep.

Papa died later that day. A day I shall always remember as the turning point in my life: November 5, 1810. I was eleven years old.

THE CURIOSITIES WILL SAVE US

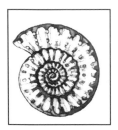 There are things one thinks will never be forgotten, but one tries to remember them, only to find that all one can recall are bits and pieces. Take Papa, for example. I thought I would always remember what Papa looked like, but when I try to conjure up an image of him now all I can remember are fragments—his thin, dark hair, his high forehead, his pale blue eyes, but not his entire face; his fine hands with their long fingers as they worked on the feathery head of a sea lily, but not his entire self. That is the way I remember the time after he died, in patches. I do not remember going to the cemetery or burying Papa, except that it was cold and raining. Oddly enough, I do remember a lot about the gathering at our house when we came back.

Fearing that Mama would be in no state to provide for the mourners, the neighbors brought cakes and ale. Mama, who had been crying and pacing the house in a daze since Papa was brought home from the beach, managed to compose herself and to listen as Uncle Philip recalled how Papa had wandered on the beach when he was a little boy. "He read in a book that nature was God's handiwork and whenever we asked him what he was doing down there, he would say he was investigating God's wonders," Uncle Philip said. He bit his lip, shook his head, and turned away so we would not see him wipe his eye.

Captain Locke, whom Papa had been visiting when he was brought back to the house that last time, consumed several glasses of ale and his red face became redder than usual, especially his nose. He stood somewhat shakily, grabbed hold of the table, and proceeded to make a speech about Papa. "He was quick, Anning was," he said, "once he set his mind to finding curiosities, he learned everything there is to know. I showed him where they were and what I knew, but he knew more than I did in no time at all. Finding things I never seen before." He shook his head sadly, paused for a second, and lifted his glass, saying, "To Richard Anning," before gulping down its contents.

Mr. Littlejohn, the stonemason, made a long rambling speech, saying how Papa was a fine craftsman, but that English craftsmen and workingmen were being squeezed and starved because of the war with Napoleon, while people of the upper classes with their land and their speculations were making money on the war. He went on at great length about the war and the French. The bit I like best came at the end of the speech. He said that Papa was an honest man who was forced by the times to turn from his original trade to another. And to

that other, the curiosities, he brought all the craftsmanship and honesty with which he had practiced furniture
making.

Not everyone who came approved of Papa. As I was
laying out the platters of food, I heard Aunt Bea, whom
I've always thought looked like a witch with her pale
face, long, thin nose, and high forehead, whisper to Mrs.
Cruikshanks, "It was the curiosities that killed him."
She looked over to Ann and John, who were standing
in their Sunday clothes with black crepe wrapped
around their sleeves, staring with bewilderment at all
the people. "If he hadn't insisted on going down to the
beach, his family wouldn't be left fatherless. But that
was all he ever thought about." Then seeing me and
realizing that I had heard her, she turned away.

She was not the only one who blamed Papa's death
on the curiosities. Later, when Lizzie and I were helping
Mrs. Cruikshanks clear up, I heard Aunt Letty Hunnicutt say to Hannah Moore, "The beach is no place for
a body. Damp, cold, and dangerous, it is. I don't understand why Molly agreed to his going down there. She
should have put a stop to it. But she was always soft,
easy to sway. She never could go up against him. He
would always have his way, no matter what a body said.
Well now, see what it's brought. Him dead and her left
with all those children to raise by herself."

"You might as well try to keep a lark from singing
as keep Mr. Anning from the beach," Lizzie said loudly

to no one in particular, silencing the two women.

"Pay no heed to those old sharp-tongued busybodies, Mary. They are spiteful and wicked, speaking of your poor dead papa that way," she said, when the two of us were alone in the scullery later. "Everyone knows it was the sea air that kept your papa going for so long." She put her hand on my arm and gazed at me with her serious gray eyes. "Poor, poor Mary. How awful for you." Suddenly I was crying and so was she.

We heard the clatter of footsteps on the stairs. Our guests were leaving. I hurriedly wiped away my tears with my handkerchief and, giving it to Lizzie so she could wipe hers, went to see them out.

Uncle Philip and Aunt Bea stayed after everyone else left to talk to Mama and Joseph about what was to become of us. I could tell that Mama was upset by the way she rushed around, pushing chairs back around the table, ordering John upstairs to bed, and Ann and I downstairs to the scullery to wash up.

Ann insisted that it was my turn to go to the pump for water, but I wanted to hear what was being said upstairs. When I reminded her that I had fetched water that morning, she said, "You're bigger and stronger, Mary, and can bring more back." Which is what she always said. I was bigger and stronger. Ann was a weak little thing, with honey-colored curls and soft brown eyes. She was a smaller version of Mama, while I look more like Papa with my dark hair, blue eyes, and high

forehead. Her shy, doubtful manner always made everyone come to her aid, including me.

"It's your turn, Ann, you are big enough now," I
replied. But when she did not go, I took pity on her as
usual and made the trip to the pump despite my desire
to hear what was being decided.

When I came back, I heard Uncle Philip say, "All
there are in the shop are his tools and a few pieces of
veneer, which you can sell, Molly."

Pointing upstairs, I shushed Ann, who was chattering
about the buns our neighbors had brought. "You forgot
the curiosities, Uncle Philip," Joseph said. "We can sell
them."

"But that's not enough to keep you, Molly," Uncle
Philip said, paying no heed to Joseph. "You'll have to
find steady work, and I'm afraid that Joseph will have
to leave Hale's and find some work that pays."

"I'd be nothing but a common workman if I left
Hale's," Joseph broke in. He sounded as if he was about
to burst into tears. "I would have no trade. . . . Papa
said. . ."

Mama interrupted him. "I do not want Joseph to
leave Hale's. Richard wanted him to have a trade. He
worked and saved to have him apprenticed, paid Hale
thirty pounds. I will not see it lost."

"The boy cannot continue with Hale," Uncle Philip
responded calmly. "You don't have the money, and
another thirty pounds is due Hale at the end of Joseph's

term. Better that Joseph leave sooner and begin to shoulder the burden of the family than later when you have nowhere to turn but the parish."

But Mama refused to be reasonable. "A thirteen-year-old lad cannot make enough to feed a family. We will come up with the thirty pounds for Hale. I will sell the sideboard Richard made to become a master crafts-man. I will sell everything if need be so that Joseph can finish the apprenticeship. You heard the lad. If he quits Hale's, all he will be is a common laborer, and there are enough of those starving around here already. If he does not learn a trade, he will not be able to provide for himself, let alone me and the children. Don't you see, Philip, the only hope we have is for Joseph to have a real trade. Otherwise we will not be able to hold up our heads. We shall be paupers."

"Molly, even if you can find the money to pay Hale at the end of Joseph's training, you need to feed the children and pay for the roof over your heads for six long years until then. How will you do that?" Uncle Philip asked.

"With the lace I make. And when there are no orders for lace, I will make whatever else I can. Ann is learning and she's a good knitter as well. We can sell her work. John will soon be able to work, too. He will be able to make himself useful somewhere. Mary has the curiosi-ties. It was you who saw to that. We will rent out the attic to people who come to take the waters in summer, we will rent out Richard's shop, we will make out," she replied. "I trust in the Lord, and I know he will care for us. Is it not written, 'Take therefore no thought for the morrow: for the morrow shall take thought for the things of itself. Sufficient unto the day is the evil thereof'?"

There was nothing Uncle Philip could reply to this.

The next morning Ann and I walked with Uncle Philip and Aunt Bea to the top of the town before parting. On the way past the marketplace Aunt Bea stopped to buy some ribbon. Uncle Philip, Ann, and I continued on our own up Broad Street past the fine houses with their tall windows. Ann skipped ahead and Uncle Philip put his arm around my shoulder. "I am afraid, Mary, my dear," he said, "that a heavy burden has been placed upon you; too heavy, perhaps. Your brother's fate depends upon your ability to find and sell curiosities. Indeed the fate of all of your family depends on that. It is foolishness to place such a burden on a lass your age. But I wish you well, my dear. I wish you well, for your sake, for your poor Mama's, and for little Ann and John's."

Despite Uncle Philip's misgivings, I was not afraid of my new responsibility, probably because I did not understand what it would mean. I was proud that everyone was depending on me, especially Joseph. I would not let him down. I had no doubt that the curiosities would provide for us.

In the days following Papa's burial Mama kept us shut up in the house. As soon as I had permission to leave the house again, I went out to look for curiosities. I did not find many that day, but as I was returning from the beach, I met a beautiful lady in a black jacket with small brass buttons who asked if she might see what I found. Attracted by her, several boys who were playing nearby gathered around us.

"Where did you find it?" she asked me, admiring a large ammonite with a fernlike pattern etched on its surface.

"In the Lias over there." I pointed down the beach to the cliffs.

"Do you find many?" she asked me.

"She makes her living selling them," Adam Garrison answered for me. "She's the Stone Girl."

"A curious curiosity," William Trowbridge added. The boys laughed.

"I shall give you a half a crown for it," said the lady, holding the ammonite up to look at it more closely.

Adam Garrison let out a long whistle.

"I'll go down to the beach and find you a dozen more for that," William Trowbridge offered.

There were other rude remarks, but I paid them no heed because I knew that despite their brave talk they were unlikely to find anything as good. She gave me the coin, which I accepted with a curtsy.

I ran all the way to Mama with the half crown. It

was more than anyone ever paid Papa for an ammonite. It was enough money to pay for bread, butter, and even tea and sugar for a week.

Mama cried for joy and hugged me hard, holding me for a long time. Recovering herself, she wiped the tears from her cheeks and began to scurry around the kitchen, putting things away. Then stopping abruptly, she ordered Ann to fetch some buns from the baker's. When we were eating them at supper that evening, she asked me to tell her again about the lady in the black spencer and how she gave me a half crown for a curiosity, which I did, except for the part about the boys and their rude remarks. She repeated the story herself every time a neighbor asked how we were getting on in the days that followed. With every telling, Mama and I grew more convinced that we could manage.

A COSTLY MISTAKE

 I soon discovered that a half crown does not go far when there are four people to feed and keep warm, nor are ladies who pay a half crown for an ammonite encountered often. Most importantly, I quickly learned that if we were to survive, I had to find curiosities and sell them all the time. With these discoveries, finding curiosities soon changed from a game to a necessity that required all my energy, ingenuity, and skill. On a particularly unsuccessful day, when I was about to give up and return home empty-handed after hours of searching, I spied a new slide further down the beach. It was growing late and the tide had long since turned, but driven by need, I went over to see what it might contain. It was a rich slide and within a few minutes I had found a sea lily. The next thing I knew the water was lapping at my heels. I'll get wet, I thought, annoyed at myself for being foolish. I began to walk back along the beach toward town.

But my way was barred by the rising tide. I did not get very far before the waves were threatening to sweep me off my feet as they came rushing in, one on the heels of the other. There was no way for me to escape except by climbing up over the cliffs, which rose up in front of me like a wall. I searched the face of the cliffs, looking for a way to climb up out of the reach of the water. I ran through the surf, looking frantically, seeking some softening in the almost perpendicular wall of rock.

At last I spied what looked like a ledge, really only a small indentation in the cliff. I scrambled up to it with difficulty and looked down. The waves were crashing at the base of the cliff, but I was out of their reach.

I clung to that spot, thinking that I was safe and could remain there until the tide receded. Then, without warning, a large wave came crashing at my feet. The tide was continuing to rise. In sheer terror, I crawled up the face of the cliff, like a fly on a wall, finding a toehold and then pulling the rest of my body up to it with the aid of the projecting rocks. Each move was an agony. I cut my hands on the sharp rock and ripped my skirt. A slippery piece of shale almost made me fall.

At last, having reached a place where I could stand, I stopped to catch my breath. I looked down. The ledge I had first stood on was covered by water now, and still the waves seemed to be mounting. How high would they go? I was afraid to think.

Desperately scanning the cliff, I looked for some way that I might get out of reach of the waves. High above me there were some bushes clinging to the cliff's face. Looking up at them I realized that those bushes meant safety. The water did not reach that high or else they would not grow there. I had to get up to them.

I began my slow crawl up the face of the cliff again. I pulled myself from projecting stone to projecting stone, creeping higher and higher. As I came up to the level of the bush that had been my goal, I grabbed hold of its trunk to pull myself up further. It pulled out of the cliff in my hand, sending me sliding down. I screamed in terror. Pummeled by falling dirt and rock, I was certain I was falling to my death. But after a moment or two, I realized that I had stopped sliding. Gradually the rocks and dirt stopped falling. I heard someone yelling, "Hold on! Hold on!" Clinging to the rock with my entire being, I lifted my head to look up.

Several feet above me and a little to one side, were two men leaning over a ledge looking down at me. With a start I recognized one of them as our neighbor Mr. Peel. "Don't be frightened. You've stopped falling," he reassured me.

Then after a minute or two, he asked, "Do you think you can get back up again?"

I nodded weakly. He guided me step-by-step back up the cliff, telling me where to put my feet, coaxing me on. When I was near the ledge on which the two men were standing, Mr. Peel took me by one arm and the other man, who had not spoken, took me by the other and pulled me up.

No sooner was I standing on the ledge beside him,

than Mr. Peel gruffly demanded, "What are you doing here, lass?"

"I was caught by the tide," I explained, brushing the dirt from my face and hair.

"Working down there by yourself, were you?" he asked.

I nodded, too exhausted to wonder what he was doing in this unlikely place.

"Well, you had better move on now and hurry home," he said. "This is no place for you now. We are expecting a ship before the tide turns."

His friend cleared his throat nervously.

Mr. Peel laughed. "Don't be shy of her, Isaac," he said, looking at me. "She's a good lass. Carrying on her father's trade. Mr. Anning was often out on the cliffs and knew to keep his mouth shut. You could trust him not to see what he wasn't meant to."

I was relieved that it was Mr. Peel on the cliff. Some other lookout landing a smuggled cargo would have been afraid to help me and would have left me to slide down the cliff.

I had barely caught my breath when Mr. Peel told Isaac to escort me to the top of the cliff. Isaac, who was a long-legged young man with a dark gypsy look, started off without even looking back to see that I was following. He made his way up the cliff with an expertise born of practice. I scrambled behind as best I could, keeping sight of the green ribbon on his cap. When he reached a bare spot that looked like a path, he stopped to wait for me to catch up. "This will take you to the top," he said, and without so much as another glance in my direction, he left me to make my way home.

It was not until I reached the streets of Lyme that I allowed myself to think about how close to drowning I had come. I shivered with the thought. I knew how Mama would carry on if she knew and decided not to say a word about what had happened.

Ordinarily, I emptied my basket when I returned to the shop and cleaned the curiosities. But on that day I was overcome by exhaustion from my ordeal on the cliffs and I did not think about the curiosity basket. I brushed myself off, turned my skirt so that the tear was covered by my apron, and went directly upstairs to warm myself by the fire.

Ann was sitting near the window knitting under Mama's watchful eye and John was sitting by the hearth playing jackstraws. "You moved that one," I said, watching him pick a straw from the jumble of straws on the hearth.

"Play with me, Mary," he begged. "Everyone is busy but me, and it's no fun picking up straws by myself." I was only too glad to lose myself in a game.

The next day was Wednesday, the day the coach came to the Three Cups Inn with its load of travelers and visitors to town. It was not until I was down in the shop that I realized that I did not have the curiosity basket with yesterday's finds and my tools. My mind raced over the events of the preceding day. Where had I put them down? I had them when I scrambled up to my first resting place on the cliff, that much I remembered, but beyond that I had no recollection of them at all. I would have to go back to look for them as soon as the coach left, as frightening as that might be. This time I would make certain that the tide was out.

The press of work did not allow me to dwell on my loss. I did not have many curiosities prepared, and there was only time to prepare one more, which I did as quickly as I could with the few tools left in the shop.

Time flew by as I worked and soon the church bell chimed two o'clock, the signal for me to put curiosities out on the table we kept outside the shop to attract travelers. Try as I might, the table looked bare. I searched through the shop for more attractive curiosities, but I could find only verteberries. I swept the whole lot of them into my apron and carried them to the table. There were eight of them—laid out in a row I thought that they looked as if they might belong together. As I was laying them out I recalled a conversation Papa and I had once had about verteberries. I had asked him if there were dragons in England. "Mr. Whitecomb says that the verteberries are the backbones of a dragon," I explained, mentioning the name of a prominent member of our meeting.

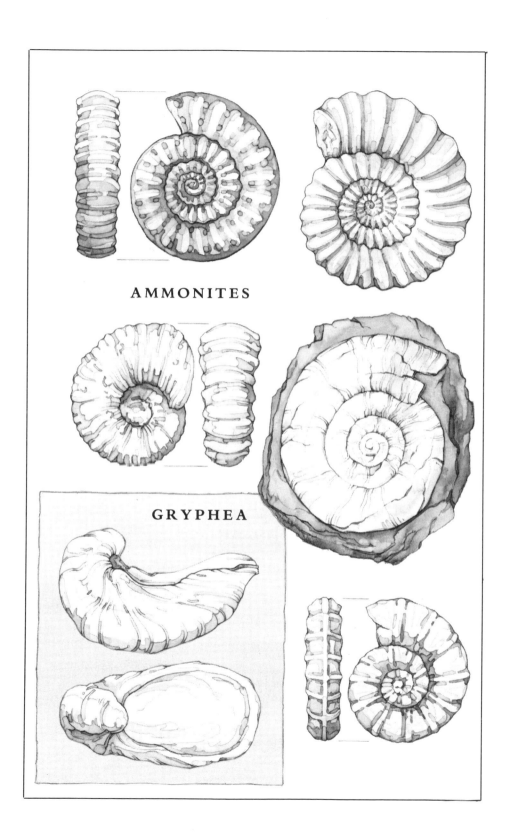

AMMONITES

GRYPHEA

Papa had smiled at my question. "Some say that. Others say they belong to a crocodile. Whatever beast they are from, it was a big one. And it lived long ago, maybe even before the flood. No one has ever seen a crocodile or a dragon in England in our time. But you never know, Mary, you never know. There are strange things on this earth.

"Mr. Johnson, from Bristol, he's interested in the verteberries we find in the cliffs. I asked him what creature they came from. He has been to university, but he does not know. Says no one does. We don't have enough pieces of the beast to know yet, but someday we will."

"How would they know if all the pieces came from the same creature?" I asked him. "They are all a jumble when we find them. Could be several different creatures mixed up together."

"Johnson tells me that collectors and scientists have their way of working these things out. But I tell him, they could be wrong and never know. Best thing is to find a skeleton in one piece. Then you know what it is. 'Well,' says he, 'Find it, Anning, find it.' "

The sound of iron wheels and horses' hooves brought me back to the present with a start. An elegant carriage had come to a stop right in front of me. A footman dressed in livery was shouting to me, "Tell Anning that Squire Henley is here."

"Mr. Anning died in November, sir," I said.

"But this is Anning's curiosity table, is it not?" he asked.

I nodded.

At that moment, Squire Henley reached over the carriage door with his cane and knocked on the side to be let out. The footman, a round, short-legged man, rolled himself down from his perch in back and went to help the Squire out of the carriage.

Squire Henley was an impressive-looking man—dressed in the old manner with knee britches instead of trousers and powdered hair—he was tall, with dark, quick eyes set in a square-jawed face. "Did I hear you say that Anning is dead?" he asked, striding over to the curiosity table. Without waiting for me to answer, he picked up a curiosity and examined it.

"Yes, sir," I answered with a curtsy.

"But then whose curiosities are these?"

"They are mine, sir. I am his daughter."

"You mean to tell me, lass, that you go down to the shore and dig these fossils out yourself?"

"Yes, sir."

He picked up a verteberrie, then another, examining all of them in turn. "Where did you get these vertebrae?"

It was the first time I had heard the word said that way, and I repeated it in order to remember it. Squire Henley must have thought that I was asking a question because he then said, "They are pieces of the backbone of an animal. I have never seen so many like these at one time. They're part of a large animal by the looks of them. Larger than anything that lives around here now. Could be a crocodile. People say there are fossil crocodiles. If you find one, lass, you tell me. Promise now. I'll pay handsomely for it."

Here I had just been thinking about what Papa had said about the dragon or the crocodile, or whatever it was, and now Squire Henley was talking about it. How strange, I thought.

Squire Henley returned to his carriage without waiting for me to reply. "I will stop by from time to time as I did with your father," he called to me. "He used to save the more interesting fossils for me, and I wish you to do the same. None of your thunderbolts, now. It is your rare ones I am interested in." And with that the carriage drove away.

I stood there daydreaming of finding the dragon for some time before I realized that the Squire had not bought anything from me. The coach was long past due. I rearranged the curiosities that he had jumbled and waited. I waited until it was late, too late to go down to the beach to hunt for my curiosity basket. No one else came past my display.

It was raining when we woke up the next morning. "Don't be foolish, child, people don't buy curiosities in this kind of weather," Mama said, when I started to put the curiosity table out. I spent the rest of the day in the workshop, preparing the few curiosities I had in the shop. But there was not much I could do with only one hammer, a medium-sized chisel, a penknife, and a mounted pin.

I stole out of the shop as soon as the rain stopped and made my way down the beach to the slide where I had so foolishly lingered. Washed away by the tides and the rain, it was much smaller than it had been. Luckily, the tide was receding, which gave me plenty of time to search for my basket. I thought I remembered where I climbed off the beach. I tried to scramble up the cliff there but only slid back down because it was so slippery from the rain.

Back down on the beach, I stopped to look around me. Was I in the right place? Then I remembered that at first I tried to walk back to town along the beach. Only when I realized that it was too late did I scramble up the cliff. I walked back along the beach searching for the place I had started my climb, but no piece of the cliff stood out from any other. There were the bushes, I remembered, searching the cliff face for some overhanging bushes, but I could see that there were bushes sprouting from several places. It was hopeless. I was close to tears in despair.

I reasoned that it was better to start my search at the top of the cliff and work my way down. Walking toward town, I spied my basket lying on the shore, tangled in a clump of seaweed. I hurried toward it with a sense of relief, only to find that the basket was empty. The tools were gone, buried in the sand or beneath the water, sunk of their own weight. I would never find them.

When I came home Mama was sitting by the window, working on lace for a wedding veil. Aunt Hunnicutt found her the work on the promise that it would be finished in two months' time. She wasn't to be paid until she delivered it.

"The coach was here," Mama said as I came in, "but they were not interested in curiosities. Didn't even bother to look. It's when the sun is shining that people are reminded of the seashore and curiosities. We're going to have to think of something to tide us over until then."

I was hungry, and I went to the sideboard.

Seeing me, Mama said, "If you eat the bread now, there will not be enough for supper."

I closed the sideboard door without taking anything.

When I was sitting with Mama, darning stockings a few days later, I said something to Mama about being cold. She told me to put a blanket around my shoulders.

"A blanket won't warm my fingers," I complained. "They are stiff from the cold and I am being clumsy."

"You cannot let a little cold discourage you, child. Just don't think about it," Mama advised. "See, I am still working the lace, and my hands are no warmer than yours. Summer will be here soon enough, and then we

will all be warm. It is summer when the money is to
be made here. We will whitewash the upstairs and take
in lodgers. And the curiosities always do better in the
summer when people come to take the waters." Why
didn't I tell Mama that I had been caught by the tide
and lost my tools and finds? I was not so much afraid
of being punished as I was ashamed. Mama, Joseph, and
the little ones were counting on me to keep us going.
My carelessness had put everyone in jeopardy. I prayed
that I would somehow be able to work round the loss
so that no one ever need know. I did not want to fail
them.

OUR LOSSES

 It was April when Ann, who had just celebrated her eighth birthday, became sick with a sore throat and a raging fever. We tried to get water down her parched throat, but she could not swallow. We bathed her burning body in cool water. Still the fever raged, convulsing her body and jerking her arms and legs. Frightened by Ann's turn for the worse, we called in Dr. Carpenter. There was little he could do. She fell unconscious and lay insensible for a day before she was delivered from her suffering into the hands of God.

While Ann lay unconscious, John, who was almost six, was taken by the same illness. He fought it for several days. On the fourth day he sat up suddenly and called for Ann, who had been his constant companion and playmate. "Why doesn't she come?" he asked.

I turned away, unable to tell him.

He saw that I was crying. "Why is Mary crying?" he asked Mama, who had come to take her turn at his bedside.

"Because Ann has gone to heaven," Mama said.

John lay back down, turned his face to the wall, and

closed his eyes. Mama thought he was sleeping. Thinking that the crisis was over, we were relieved. The next morning his fever rose again and by evening he, too, was dead.

"You've taken my husband, my daughter, and now my son. Take me. Do not leave me behind! I have nothing left to hope for. Take me so that I may be with them!" Mama cried out when she saw that John was dead.

"Mama, Mama, I'm here," I said, putting my arms around her. She threw me off and I fell to the floor, where I sat watching as she howled in grief. "Why? Why? My babies! My babies are gone! Gone!" I didn't know what to do. I was afraid to leave her to go for help.

Mrs. Cruikshanks, who was passing by, heard her cries, and guessing that something terrible had happened, came in. "Get up, child. Go, fetch Joseph and the doctor," she ordered, setting me in motion.

It was our neighbors' kindness that carried us through the next days. They had laid out Ann when she died, and now they laid out John. They were patient with Mama, who would not be comforted in her grief. They had kind words for Joseph and me. They ordered the coffins and arranged for the burial.

In the spring, with the trees and fields clothed in new green, we gave Ann and John to our Father in heaven, who in his divine wisdom had gathered them unto himself.

We had barely enough money to pay for Ann and John's burial and none to pay Dr. Carpenter. "There is nothing for it but to apply to the parish for aid," Mr. Cruikshanks told Joseph.

Joseph refused to hear such talk, "It will break Mama's spirit to come down so in the world. She's grief stricken as it is," he replied. The only way Joseph could think to save us from going on the parish rolls was to leave his apprenticeship and to find work that paid immediately.

"What kind of work will you find without a trade?" Mama asked when Joseph informed her of his plan. He was silent and she answered herself, "None that pays. If you leave Hale's we will only have another hungry mouth to feed here. Our only hope is for you to become an upholsterer. Then you'll be earning good money steadily. Summer is almost here, if we can hold out until then, we'll make it up with the curiosities."

All Mama's hopes seemed to be concentrated on summer. "Things are always better in summer," Mama said to me day after day as we sat down to our dinner of bread and porridge, a monotonous diet which was only occasionally broken by a watery soup made with a few tired vegetables. We had not seen meat on our table since Papa died. "We shan't have to spend as much on coal when summer comes, and of course you shall be bringing in more," she repeated. "Your poor, dear Papa always did better with the curiosities in summer, what with the travelers and all."

I listened and did not reply. Though I continued to search the beach for curiosities day after day, I had collected little. There were no good slides that spring, and I did not have a good geological hammer or heavy chisels for breaking fossils out of the rocks. I could not bring myself to tell Mama, poor, dear Mama who had suffered so much and who still had faith and hope despite it all, that it was hopeless.

But one day when there was no money to buy bread and we had nothing to eat but porridge, which we had been eating for several days, I could not bear to listen to her go on about her hopes for the summer any longer. How could she be so blind? Didn't she see that I was not bringing home many curiosities? She passed through the workshop several times a day. Didn't she see that the tools were missing? Why did she keep saying the same foolish things again and again when we were cold and hungry and summer's coming would change little. I ran from the room, bolting down the stairs.

"Mary," Mama called down the stairs after me. "Mary, what is the matter, child?"

I did not answer. I ran frantically from shelf to work table and back to the shelves again, taking the curiosities from the shelves and carrying them to the workbench.

Alarmed, Mama came down to the workshop. "What are you doing?" she asked.

I counted the curiosities on the workbench, "One, two, three . . ." There were about thirty curiosities in all. "Thirty," I said, turning to face Mama. "Not enough, Mama. Not enough to make a difference when the visitors come next month. We cannot count on the curiosities to pay our debts or to buy our food." I turned away to rush from the shop, but before I got to the door, Mama caught me in her arms and swung me around. Pressing me to her, she held me, as I cried with shame.

When I finally stopped crying, I told her how I lost my tools. Mama was quiet when I finished my story. She held me to her and swayed gently, rocking me back and forth, back and forth. "It was wrong of me to place such a burden on one so young," she said. I wanted to say that it wasn't a burden, that it was just that I forgot myself, but Mama hushed me and held me in her arms while I cried.

We did not speak of the lost tools again. It was decided that I would go into service in a big house, where my food and bed would be provided. Mama would sell our belongings and go live with her sister, Aunt Letty Hunnicutt, and her husband, Mr. Hunnicutt, in Axminster until Joseph finished his term with Hale and was able to set up as an upholsterer. Then, God willing, we would set up house again.

Mama started a letter to Aunt Letty and Uncle Hunnicutt to ask if she might come live with them, but put the pen down after the first sentence telling of Ann and John's deaths. She left the letter lying on the table unfinished and went to sit at the window with her lacework, but she did not work. She stared out the window all that day, the next, and the day after. I cannot say how many days. I fled the house and wandered up and down the shore looking for curiosities. When I would return from my fruitless searches, Mama would turn away from the window to look at me and then would turn back to her lacework without a word. After a few stitches, her gaze would wander back to the window and her hands would grow motionless. She would forget to put out food at mealtimes. I do not know whether she ate, but we did not sit down together. We did not talk. We could not bring ourselves to. Talking would make our losses and the breakup of our family real.

Joseph, who had put out word that I was looking for a post, heard that the housekeeper at High Cliff was looking for a girl to run errands and to help the cook. High Cliff was a grand house on Pound Street where many newcomers to town were building homes. It was owned by a family that made its money in tea plantations in India. Joseph told me to go there the next morning.

How I dreaded the interview! More than that I dreaded leaving our home to go to work in a strange house and live among strangers. Lizzie and I had discussed what it would be like. Knowing that I had little choice in the matter and that I was afraid, Lizzie tried to comfort me with pictures of a kind, young mistress who would make a friend and companion of me and who would let me read her books, and take me with her to London and Bath. "Now that could be a real adventure, Mary. Going to London in the company of a young lady," she said. "She might even let you sit in on her lessons." Lizzie's gray eyes were round and solemn as she tried to convince me, but her mouth twitched and I could see that she didn't believe that such a thing was possible any more than I did.

Far more likely, I thought, as I climbed up Broad Street, was what happened to Susanne Allen. She had gone to work in a big house after her father died. We never saw her again down on Bridge Street. She did not even come when Grannie Allen, who had raised her, was buried. Her little sister, Fannie, told me that her mistress would not give her permission and had cuffed her when she cried.

The wrought-iron gate to the carriage yard was open when I arrived. I walked into the graveled courtyard. The house was large, with a portico supported by columns and wings stretching out on either side. I knew better than to call at the front door, but I could not find

the tradesmen's entrance. I walked along one wing of
the house to the side.

I was stopped by a gruff voice demanding to know
where I was going. "This is private property," the voice
warned me. I looked around for the speaker, but saw
no one.

"I'm looking for the servants' entrance," I explained,
still looking about to see who was speaking.

"Oh, come to see Mrs. Wiggins, have you? You look
a bit young to be leaving home," the voice said.

"Where are you? I cannot see you."

"Up here in the tree," the voice said.

Then I saw him high in a beech tree, a wrinkled, old
man with a long white beard, wearing a broad hat with
a saw in his hand. "The tradesmen's entrance is round
the other side of the house," he told me.

I walked back to the front of the house, past the
porticoed entrance, past the tall blank-eyed windows
that seemed to be looking down on me disapprovingly,
and around to the other side where down three steps was
a small, black door. I knocked. No one answered. I
knocked again. My heart was beating so loudly I could
barely hear anything else. After several minutes during
which I knocked repeatedly, I heard someone call
through the door, "Stop that banging!"

I called back, "It is Mary Anning, the cabinetmaker's
girl. I have come to talk to Mrs. Wiggins about running
errands." I heard the bolt being pulled.

The door opened a crack. "Wait here," said a red-faced woman in large checkered apron and white mob-cap. Then she slammed the door in my face.

I waited for several more minutes before she returned to say that Mrs. Wiggins would see me. She led me through the scullery and the kitchen into a small room with a pine table, one chair, several leather-bound account books, and a number of locked cupboards, and left me to wait there. Soon I heard a heavy tread in the hall and Mrs. Wiggins, an enormous woman dressed all in black except for a white cap, was upon me.

"You have come to see about running errands?" she asked in a booming voice as she looked down on me from her towering height.

I opened my mouth to answer. I moved my lips. But no sound issued. I nodded my head instead.

"Don't wave your head at me," she bellowed. "Answer 'yes, ma'am,' or 'no, ma'am.'"

"Yes, ma'am," I whispered.

"Speak up! You are Anning, the cabinetmaker's child?"

"Yes, ma'am," I repeated.

"The one who sells curiosities?"

My chin hurt because Mama had tied my bonnet too tightly, but I was too frightened to raise my hands to loosen the strings. "Yes, ma'am," I answered.

"I hear that you go down to the beach to look for them."

"Yes, ma'am. I sell the curiosities now that my father is dead."

She snorted at this. "And your mother permits you to wander around the beach by yourself, unchaperoned?"

I did not reply. "Answer me," she demanded, but she went on before I could. "Does she not know that there are smugglers there? Brigands? And still she allows a girl to go there. But then your family does not attend St. Michael's, does it, girl?"

"No, ma'am," I said. "We go to chapel."

"A Dissenter? No, you will not do," she said. "I cannot vouch for the morals of a girl who has been allowed to run free like you. We are respectable people here." And with that she dismissed me.

I ran all the way down Broad Street, past the proud, tall-windowed houses, through the throngs crowding the marketplace and shambles, and onto to the safety of Bridge Street in a confusion of feeling. I had escaped from Mrs. Wiggins, but her rejection still left me in need of work. I did not tell Mama why Mrs. Wiggins did not hire me. Mrs. Wiggins's disapproval of my fossil hunting would have caused her great anguish. Instead, I muttered something about there being a mistake. And Mama, who was vague about everything those days, did not inquire further. "Something will turn up soon," she said, and turned back to the window.

Not knowing what else to do, I continued to go to

the beach in search of curiosities. One day, not long afterward, as I was returning from the beach, I saw Dr. Carpenter leaving our house. Fearing the worst, I ran into the shop, and up the stairs, calling, "Mama! Mama!" I pulled the door open and stopped. Mama was not in her customary place by the window. She was kneeling by the sideboard. On the long table were dishes, salvers, mugs—the contents of the sideboard.

"I've sold the sideboard to Dr. Carpenter," Mama explained. "He is giving me a good sum for it. Now you needn't go into service, and I needn't give up our house and go to live with Mr. Hunnicutt. We can stay here together . . . for a little while longer."

I ran to her and threw my arms around her neck. "Oh, Mama," I said over and over, unable to say anything else.

"It is just a thing, a piece of furniture," Mama said, wiping her tears with the back of her hand.

But I knew that the sideboard was not just another thing. It had always meant a great deal to her. Papa made it to become a master cabinetmaker. It was the one fine thing in our house, the one thing that showed Papa's true craftsmanship. It had a bowed front with inlaid rosewood panels.

"We should not set much stock in the things of this world. I would have had to sell it anyway when Joseph finishes his term. It is just as well that Dr. Carpenter offered me the money for it now. Truth be known, he paid me more than it was worth. I do not want to take charity from him, but he insists it is not charity. He tells me that he has admired it ever since he first set eyes on it."

I did not ask her how we would pay Hale the thirty pounds due him when Joseph's apprenticeship was over. I was too relieved that I did not have to be parted from Mama and go into service to worry much about what would happen in five years. I would earn the money somehow.

SOMETHING STARES AT ME FROM THE CLIFF

 Days and weeks passed without incident. I can remember little of that hard summer, except that somehow we endured. It was November again, a year since Papa was taken from us. I was walking along Church Cliff Walk intending to make my way down to the beach. It was quite a different scene from summer when the town was filled with visitors. In June, the deep blue sea stretched out against a paler blue sky, the air was warm, and there were groups of holidaymakers strolling along Church Cliff Walk in their light summer clothes. Now it was cold. Slate-colored clouds rolled across a lead sky. Except for me, the Walk was deserted. Down on the beach waves rushed headlong crashing against the base of the cliffs, threw spray high in the air, withdrew, and crashed again. The beach was impassable. But still I stayed on the cliffs, drawn by the wild force of the sea.

The clouds grew blacker, gulls cried as they circled overhead, a raindrop splattered on my nose and then another. I turned for home. I just reached the door as a clap of thunder announced the storm. The sky opened, letting loose a torrent. It rained steadily without letup for four days and for all that time the wind blew with gale force. "A real southwester," Mama called it. I remained indoors wrapped up against the cold in Mama's wool shawl, listening to the wind driving the rain against the panes, rattling the shutters, and whistling through the eaves.

As soon as the rain let up I put on my clogs and dressed to go out collecting. "The wind is still high, and it is dangerous near the cliffs now," Mama warned.

Remembering that Papa always said that the best finds were made just after a storm, I was impatient to get down to the beach. But I soon found that Mama was right. Though the tide was out, the waves, pushed by the wind, made the beach impassable.

It was several more days before I had another chance to go down to the shore. Thrown this way and that by the waves, huge timbers, barrel staves, bricks, driftwood, seaweed, pieces of broken pottery, and even rags littered the beach. It was slow work to pick my way over them toward a new slide that looked promising.

The first thing I pulled out of the mound of clay, rock, and dirt was flat bottomed and domed on top. It might have been a fossil urchin, but I could not be sure because it was covered with sticky, wet clay. I took it over to a pool left behind by the tide and started to wash it off. As I was watching the clay cloud the water of the pool, I heard a roar and turned, in fright, only to see a mass of dirt and pieces of rock falling from the top of the cliff to the beach below. Scanning the cliff trying to decide whether it was safe for me to remain, I found myself staring at a grayish white circle with two slightly curved parallel lines beneath it. Looking at it, I had the strange feeling that it was staring back at me.

I stood there for what must have been several minutes waiting to see if more of the cliff was going to fall before I approached it to see what the circle was. Close up it was easier to see that it was a curiosity, but I did not recognize it as anything I had seen before. I took my hammer and chisel out of my pocket and gently worked the wet Lias near the circle. Set inside the large, thin circle was a smaller circle made of several bony plates, like flower petals. At the center was a hole. Could it be an eye? I wasn't sure.

I slowly worked around the lines that protruded underneath. I bared more of the fossil, but I could not make out what it was. I worked in between the two lines with a nail. There was something there. It was perpendicular to the two parallel lines. I scraped off the wet clay with mounting excitement. There was no mistaking what I saw. It was a tooth, and there was another one next to it. I had collected teeth like these near the large vertebrae. I laughed. Could it possibly be? I whirled about madly until I fell down on the sand with giddiness. When I calmed down, I looked at it again just to make certain. There was no mistake. I had found the dragon!

I put the tools back in my pocket and ran all the way back to town, jumping over all the obstacles in my way, sliding, falling, picking myself up, and running until I reached the house. I threw the door to the shop open and tore up the stairs yelling, "Mama! Mama! I found it," not realizing until I was in the house that Mama was not there.

Without stopping to catch my breath, I ran to Hale's to tell Joseph. I burst into the shop, startling poor Mr. Hale, who was on a stepladder. "Where's Joseph?" I demanded. I didn't wait for an answer, seeing him bent over an armchair. I shouted, "Joseph, I've found it! I found the dragon at the end of the Church Cliffs near the ledges."

Joseph looked at me as if I had just gone mad. "What dragon?" he asked.

"I don't know if it is a dragon or a crocodile," I said, stopping for the first time since I found it. "I don't know what it is, but it's a fossil in the cliffs, and it's big." I told him and Mr. Hale the story of my discovery from the beginning.

"You've only seen a tooth and you come bursting in here like that. I have no time for such foolishness," Mr. Hale said, turning away to fetch a bolt of cloth that he had stored in the rafters.

My certainty crumbled like dried marl. Papa and I had found other teeth like it, but we had never found an eye socket or a jaw before.

I had to make certain that it was actually there and that I had not made it all up. Quickening my pace, I passed our house, made my way back down to the beach, and over to the east end of Church Cliff. There it was, the large eye staring at me. I took out my chisel and set to work again. The fossil was in a narrow band of limestone that lay between beds of shale. Shale splits easily. That meant that getting the fossil out of the cliff might be possible. But how big was it? I worked at it and worked at, but with only my small hammer, chisel, and a nail, I could not tell.

The tide was coming in and I had no time to explore further. Reluctantly, I started for home.

"Did you find anything?" Mama asked without looking up from her lace when I came in.

"I think I've found the dragon!"

Mama, looked up from her work, staring at me uncomprehendingly.

"The what?" she asked.

"The dragon, the one people talk about. It's in the cliffs. It's really there. It's not just a story. It's a big, big curiosity, Mama. The biggest we have ever seen. Papa said I might find such a creature, and I have."

"Tell me what it is again?" Mama asked, still not understanding.

"A dragon, or maybe a crocodile," I repeated, describing the long line of teeth and the bony eye that stared at me. But it was not until the next morning, when she came with me to see the curiosity for herself, that she believed that I had found anything unusual.

"My heavens, what a thing!" she exclaimed, standing before the head.

"It's a petrified dragon or crocodile, that's what Papa said. He said that collectors talk about it. They're the ones who want the verteberries. Squire Henley made me promise that if I ever found it I would save it for him. He will pay me handsomely for it."

Mama furrowed her brow. "Are you certain that this is the creature he was talking about?"

"No, but he said the crocodile, or whatever creature it was that the verteberries belong to. I think this must be it."

She shook her head. "Well, if you say Henley told you he wanted it, I guess he does, though whatever for, I will never understand."

She stood in front of the cliff staring at the fossil for some time. Then she sighed, turned away, and started back for town. I caught up with her. "Well, what do you think?" I asked eagerly.

"You may as well not have found it for all the good it will do us. We'll never get it out of the cliff. It is too big for us, Mary. We would have to hire some work-men to help us break it out, and we do not have the money to hire them."

"I can do it, Mama. I know I can."

She shook her head. "I do not mean to be discouraging, child, but it would be a waste of your time even trying. Besides, we do not have the tools for such a job."

"But Mama," I pleaded, "it will fetch a lot of money. We cannot just let it remain in the cliff."

Mama nodded wearily at my arguments, but did not reply.

I was not to be discouraged. I believed with all my being that if I tried hard enough and did not give up, I would have that fossil. Looking back now, I can see that it was unreasonable for a twelve-year-old girl with only a hammer and one not very heavy chisel to expect to cut a fossil almost as big as she was out of the cliff. But then I am not only Papa's child, I am also Mama's. When one cannot accept what is reasonable, one must have faith and hope to fly in face of what reason denies.

However, I do admit that faith and hope are only a beginning. Despite hours and hours of work chipping away at the rock, I made little progress until spring when Mr. Hale was ill and Joseph had the free time to help me. It was he who thought of borrowing a pick, crowbars, proper square-headed hammers, a mallet, heavier chisels, and wedges from the stonemason.

At first Mr. Littlejohn was reluctant to let us use his tools for such a "foolish project." Finally he relented, saying that it was only because we were Richard Anning's children that he was letting us use them. But he still could not understand what we wanted with a stone monster. He became more enthusiastic when he came down to the beach to see for himself. Standing before it, he shook his head and laughed, saying that he was glad it was stone and not wandering around Lyme today.

Once we had the proper tools, extracting the fossil began in earnest. The rhythmic clink of our hammers hitting our chisels filled the air as we chipped away at the cliff. The creature was embedded in limestone surrounded by shale beds that splintered under our blows and fell to the ground at our feet where it lay in mounds. But still the fossil remained in place. The more rock we broke, the more there seemed to be to break. My back ached and my arms hurt from pounding at the rock so much that I cried with fatigue, but still I continued and so did Joseph. Then, at last, after hours and days of slow difficult work, we had a deep enough channel around the skull so that we could start to break it out using metal wedges.

When we had gotten this far Joseph's friends, Robert Whitesides and John Whittle, came to help. They had never collected curiosities and knew nothing about getting them out of the cliff. "Don't get too close to the curiosity," I cautioned them, remembering Papa's advice to me. "Angle your tools well away from it. Be certain to get all of it."

All of it, as it turned out after we had pried the fossil out of the rock with crowbars, was only the head of the dragon. But what a head it turned out to be! It was four feet long, as big as an eight-year-old child, with a snout filled with sharp teeth that ran almost its entire length.

If that was the head, how much bigger must the body have been, I thought. But to my bitter disappointment the body was not where I expected it to be.

AN ACCIDENT LEADS TO A DISCOVERY

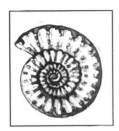 No sooner did we have the head laid out in the workshop than all the neighbors and friends from our quarter of Lyme came to see for themselves "the monster's head" that the Anning children brought back from the beach. They crowded into the tiny shop, joking and jostling one another. It was an amazing scene, one which I don't think I'll ever forget.

"I wouldn't have such a thing in my house," Mr. Cruikshanks said, poking it with his pipe. "Wouldn't be able to sleep knowing there was a dragon there."

" 'Fraid it might come to life, John?" asked Mr. Adams, with a guffaw.

"You never know," Mr. Cruikshanks replied. "Now that it's not buried in the cliff, it might come back to life. I heard such stories, things people thought were gone, come back. . . ."

Mrs. Cruikshanks gave Mr. Cruikshanks a withering look. "Told over a glass of brandy, no doubt," she commented.

Mr. Halowell the jailer, who came in from the jail next door with his round little wife, poked his finger in the monster's mouth and exclaimed, "Did you ever see such a mouthful of teeth?"

"You could borrow some for your own mouth, Rob. I don't think the beast would miss them," his wife told him, much to everyone's amusement.

I was flushed with happiness at all of this attention. I told them that in cleaning away the stone from around the fossil's teeth, I had found that it had teeth in different stages of growth, which made me think that it grew new teeth to replace the old.

"Wish I could do the same," Mr. Halowell replied, laughing at himself.

Of course Lizzie, who was my closest friend, came. She had been to the beach when we were working on extracting the fossil. Now she came to see the fossil laid out in the shop, bringing Caroline Gleed and Jane Lovett along. Despite their contempt for me and for my fossil hunting, Caroline and Jane were eager to see "the monster's head" that everyone else in our quarter of town was talking about.

"My brother says that it is so ugly it must belong to the devil," Caroline said, pushing past me and going directly to the fossil. Seeing it, she gasped, and stepped back. "He's right. It is ugly. A monster!" Then turning to me, she said, "You must be the only girl in all of England who could find such a thing, Mary."

"The only girl who is queer enough to want to," commented Jane, loud enough so that I could hear.

Struggling to keep my temper, I answered, "No one has ever found such a fossil before. We don't really know what it is."

"Fossil?" Lizzie asked. She, like almost everyone in Lyme then, called them curiosities.

"A fossil is a curiosity," I explained.

"Any fool can see that it is a petrified monster," Jane said.

Trying to salvage the situation, Lizzie said, "Some people say that it is the head of a crocodile."

"It does look something like the pictures of crocodiles," I admitted. "That's what Squire Henley called it."

"Whatever it is, be glad it does not live in England now," Jane said. And with that she and Caroline turned away and left the shop.

This upset Lizzie, who, despite all of her efforts to smooth things over, was caught once again between me and others. "I should have known better than to bring them here. But everyone was talking about your find, and they wanted to see it. They said they wouldn't come unless I came with them. They think you hate them, Mary. I told them that you didn't hate them at all, it is just that you are interested in other things. I hoped that by bringing them here I would be able to convince them."

"Hate them, Lizzie? It is they who hate me. I know you meant no harm in bringing them. You have always tried to smooth my way with them. But they have made

up their minds that I am strange and contemptible, and it doesn't matter what I do."

"They are just jealous"—Lizzie dismissed them—"and rude. I don't care what Caroline and Jane say about your crocodile. It is wonderful that you have been able to get it out of the cliffs. It should give an enormous boost to your trade, Mary. Everyone will want to see it, and when they do, they will want curiosities of their own. You wait and see. I'll even warrant that when curiosities are all the rage, Caroline and Jane will change their opinion of you. But you must promise, Mary, that you will be friendly and kind."

"Haven't I just been friendly?" I asked her indignantly.

"Yes, you have," she admitted, "but still, Mary . . ." She did not finish, but I knew she thought I was being proud even if she would not say it. Instead, she repeated her prediction that fossils were sure to be the rage when people heard the news.

She was right. The discovery of the crocodile head did give an enormous boost to my curiosity trade. The news of my find spread from our quarter of town to the marketplace and from there up Broad Street and through the town to the visitors who were always looking for something to amuse themselves. They thronged into our little shop so that I barely had room to move or time to work on preparing my finds. "You should charge them a halfpenny to take a look," one of the coachmen who drove through Lyme advised. "That's what they do in London. They've this place there where you can see all sort of things, and they charge a halfpenny to go in. This here dragon head you have here is better'n anything they have there. Let people pay for a look, and in no time you shall have some real money."

But I could not bring myself to ask for even as little as a halfpenny to see the crocodile's head. I liked the visitors and gawkers, and I loved their admiration. "It was a lass who found it. Just turned thirteen," I heard one woman say, and I puffed up with pride.

Besides, those who came to look often stopped to buy the smaller curiosities I had for sale. In fact, I could barely keep up with the demand for curiosities, although I was becoming more successful than I had been in finding them. Suddenly everyone was interested in them. Usually the visitors began by thinking they could find curiosities themselves, and they went to the beach with geological hammers and chisels, bought from Mr. Adams's blacksmith shop. But when they found curiosity hunting more difficult than they expected, they came to buy mine. And for the first time since Papa's death we did not have to count every penny to see if we had enough to pay for bread. We even had enough to ask Mr. Adams to make some heavy chisels and hammers to replace the ones I lost.

The one person who did not come to see the croco-

dile head that busy summer of 1812 was the one person
I most wanted to come: Squire Henley. I sent a message
to Colway Manor that I had found the head of a crocodile and was saving it for him. But I received no reply.
A day or two later, I learned from one of the manor's
gardeners that the master was away.

I was disappointed of course, but I told myself it was
all for the best, and allowed myself to hope that I would
succeed in finding the body of the fossil before the
squire's return and then have the entire creature for him.

I thought about finding the body all the time. It stood
to reason that it was not far from where I found the
head. But "not far" covered a lot of ground. The body
could be in the sixty-five-foot-high cliffs that rise from
the beach, under the beach, or even farther out, underwater. It would take a lifetime or more to search all of
those places thoroughly.

I will not bother to write about all the false hopes
and heartbreaks of my search. Like all quests, mine had
its full measure of failure. But in the end, what I remember is the success. It was because of an accident that I
saw something that was right in front of me that I had
not been seeing before. Seeing this led me to see something else that I hadn't noticed before, and once I had
realized this, I knew where to look for the rest of the
crocodile.

To stretch the time I had for collecting, I was in the
habit of going to the beach just as the tide started out.

To keep from being swamped, I ran along the base of the cliffs from one high point to the next in the pauses between the waves, arriving at my destination wet from the spray but in time to start looking just as the water was receding.

One day I misjudged a wave, and it swept me off my feet. I paddled as best I could in my clogs and heavy skirt while holding on to my bag of tools, trying to regain my footing. Another wave came, knocking me down, filling my mouth and nose with water, and dragging me so that I lost my clogs. My arms, stomach, and legs were scratched and bruised. I was certain that I was drowning. But only seconds later, the crest of the wave passed me by, leaving me behind in calmer water. As I struggled to stand, another wave swept me toward the cliffs, gently depositing me at their base, my tool bag clutched in my hand.

Stunned and gasping, I watched the wave that had carried me in rushing back out to sea, stirring up the gravel as it went. Then I looked round for my clogs. I spotted them a little way off, sticking out of the gravel. I pulled them out. Then I began to wonder where had all this gravel come from? The beach is usually covered with large pebbles, not gravel. Where were the pebbles? Could they have been washed away by the tide?

With my clogs back on my feet, I hastened along the beach to some high ground. As I waited for the tide to recede a little more, I watched the waves come in to shore and pull back again. I realized that the pebbles were too big to be washed away. More likely they were lying buried beneath the gravel. And if they were beneath the gravel, what else might the gravel be covering?

As soon as the tide was out far enough for me to get down the beach, I made my way there and began digging. I had no spade or shovel and could only dig with my bare hands. I dug until the hole I made was as long as my arm and still I had not reached the pebbles. But I knew that they had to be there. I returned the next day with a shovel and pickax. I dug a trench along the base of the cliff where I found the head and then proceeded to enlarge it. I dug for several feet before I reached the layer of pebbles. I threw the shovel aside and, jumping into the hole I had made, started to cast the pebbles aside. Below a shallow layer of pebbles, no more than two feet deep, I came to the Lias, the same Lias as the cliffs. I continued enlarging the area that I uncovered, but found nothing before the trench I was in began to fill with water.

I found the body at the end of the third day of digging. Before I had a chance to do more than uncover a few vertebrae, the tide began to move back in and I had to stop work. No matter, I thought, the beast would not move before I returned for it.

Mama and I celebrated that evening with a dinner of

sausages, potatoes, and ale. "Can you imagine the look on the squire's face when he hears of this?" Mama asked as she put the sausages in the pan. "He probably never thought it would be found. What do you think he'll pay for it?"

"Thirty pounds, maybe forty," I guessed, naming what seemed like fantastic sums.

"Something handsome, I suppose," Mama continued, hardly hearing my answer. "We will put it aside to pay Hale when Joseph's term is finished. Then we won't have to worry about that anymore. Won't that be nice?"

"We might have some left over," I joined in, "then we shall have meat on Sunday. Not every Sunday mind you, but special Sundays. We might even have enough to buy bacon every so often, or better yet, sticky buns. I love sticky buns." I went on making plans as I inhaled the aroma of frying sausages.

We were soon brought back to reality. The next morning when I went to Mr. Littlejohn's to see if I might borrow his tools for the job, he predicted that I would never get the body of the fossil out. "The tide will go out, you'll work like a slave and uncover a bit, then the tide'll be right back in, covering it up again. If you insist on trying, you're welcome to them, but they'll do you no good against the power of the tide."

I thought that he was only talking that way because he was a sour old man, jealous of our good fortune. But in the days that followed I discovered how right he was. Neither my strength nor Joseph's was a match for the tide. We borrowed from the sum set aside to pay the house tax to hire a laborer from a nearby farm, but even with his help we could not uncover enough of the body to get it out before the incoming tide undid our work.

It was in late October, almost a year from the time I first discovered the crocodile head, and I was walking on the beach one afternoon after a storm. I slipped and with my arms flailing the air as I tried to recover my footing, I realized that I was walking on pebbles, not gravel. The heavy blanket of gravel covering the pebbles had been washed away by the autumn tides and currents.

Trying to hold back my excitement, I made my way as quickly as I could to the place where I left the crocodile's body. I dug down through the thin layer of pebbles until I came to the Lias. The vertebrae and ribs were still there, lying embedded in the Lias. Now with the beach lower than it had been during the summer, getting the body out seemed possible. All I needed was help.

Joseph suggested that we hire workmen from the quarry to get the body out of the rock. They would know all there was to know about cutting rock, and they would have the proper tools. Once again we borrowed from the money set aside to pay the house tax.

Mama was afraid, after all the disappointments, that

we would not succeed in getting the body out of the rock, and that we would be left short when it was time to pay the taxes on the cottage. She fussed a great deal as I set off for the quarry, giving me all sorts of advice. "Offer them a half crown for the job. We might go as high as a crown, but we'll offer one-half to start with and see how far we can get. Pay the head man a shilling to begin work, and pay him the remainder when they get the curiosity out of the rock, and not before."

The first person I saw at the quarry was a boy about my age who was sitting on the ground outside a small windowless lean-to, peeling the bark from a stick with a penknife. "I'd like to speak to the man in charge here," I told him. The boy continued cutting at the bark. "I've a job for him and some of the workmen," I said, trying to sound as if I hired workmen every day. Still the boy did not respond.

I saw a group of men working some way off near a stack of limestone slabs, and I approached them. A man, who was covered from head to toe in a fine, white dust, detached himself from the group and slowly made his way over to me. "What is it you want, lass?" he asked.

"I've a job for some men," I told him.

"And what kind of a job would a young 'un like you have?" he asked.

I told him that I needed his help getting something out of the Lias on the beach, deciding not to confuse him with talk of dragons or crocodiles.

"The beach is a dangerous place to work," he said, taking his cap off to reveal his dark, unpowdered hair.

I told him that I worked there, hoping to raise his pride.

"That you are willing to put yourself in danger is none of my affair," he said, turning back to the limestone. But he only took a few steps before he stopped and asked, "What is it you want us to cut out of the rock?"

"A curiosity," I said, adding that I was in the business of selling them.

He laughed at this, a big, hearty laugh, as if it was the most amusing thing he'd ever heard.

I could feel myself growing warm, and I drew myself up and said, "I am willing to pay for your help, sir." At the mention of pay he stopped laughing. "How much?"

When I told him I would pay a half crown, he shook his head, "Now how does a lass like you have a half crown?" he asked.

I stated my terms: one shilling to begin with and the rest when the curiosity was out of the rock. I took the coin out of my pocket to show him that I was in earnest.

"A half crown may not be enough," he said. "It depends on how many workmen you'll need and for how long."

I said that I would need four men for two days, three days at the most.

"Four men for two or three days will cost you more

than a half crown," he replied. After much back and forth he agreed that for four shillings I might purchase the labor of four men with their tools.

The appointed day arrived. It was clear, with a pale, cloudless sky. I led the four men who were waiting for me at the foot of the Church Cliff path to the place where the crocodile lay. With much bantering and joking about the "treasure" that they were going to unearth for the lass, they set to work moving the pebbles aside. With four of them it did not take long to uncover the body. No sooner did they discover that my treasure really existed than their manner changed. "Did you ever see such a beast?" the headman asked.

The others only shook their heads in amazement at its size.

I did not want it taken out of the rock that immediately surrounded it because I was afraid it would crumble. I advised them that the skeleton was stuck in the Lias like a boiled fish's skeleton lying in its own jelly. "You have to cut it away from the platter. Cut behind it deep enough so you don't disturb it," I said.

"It's too big. It will crumble just from its own weight," the headman protested.

I suggested that we carve it out in sections, marking off each cut.

"Well, let's go to it," the headman commanded. "The lass knows her business. Now it's our turn to show her we know ours."

First they built a barrier out of pilings to keep the pebbles from being washed back by the tide. Then they set to work cutting the fossil out of the Lias. The ring of their chisels and hammers on the Lias was deafening.

The weather held for the first two days, but on the third day when we were almost finished, the sky was ominous. It was absolutely black by the time we had struggled up the cliff with a slab of rock containing ribs and vertebrae four feet long, weighing several hundred pounds. A small crowd of eager onlookers was waiting for us when we returned to the beach for the second section. They helped us roll the second piece of the body onto the litter. The first drops of rain were falling as we carried the litter up the cliff. By the time we returned to the beach for the tail section, the rain was coming down steadily, but no one seemed to mind. When the quarrymen hoisted the tail onto the litter there was a loud cheer from the onlookers.

The workmen carrying the litter were followed by a procession of onlookers as they made their way up the cliff from the beach. And what a procession it was! Undaunted by the rain, everyone from sailors who had just landed at the Cobb, to fishermen, artisans, working-men, apprentices, and schoolboys joined the parade that wound past the churchyard of St. Michael's, past the old half-timbered houses on Church Street onto Bridge Street to our little cottage, gaily chanting:

The crocodile!
The crocodile is a mighty beast,
That lives in summer climes.

One got lost,
And covered with frost,
Found its way to Lyme.

I had cleared the workshop in preparation for the crocodile's body, but even so there was not enough room in the shop to lay the pieces end to end. Including the head, the crocodile measured almost seventeen feet. It was by far the largest fossil anyone had ever seen.

NEW PLACES,
UNCOMFORTABLE THOUGHTS

Rereading what I have written thus far, I can see that, once Papa set me on my course, my life before the discovery of the crocodile seems straightforward enough. Of course there were difficulties, but they were difficulties that might be expected. It was after I found the crocodile that my life took some unexpected turns and my path became tangled.

A notice of the discovery of the fossil crocodile was printed in the *Sherborne Mercury* on November 9, 1812. After it ran the collectors started to appear in the shop. Among those who came, the person who has influenced me the most is Miss Elizabeth Philpot. She and her sister Margaret Philpot are said to have one of the best collections of curiosities in all of England. I had met the Philpot sisters in Papa's shop and seen them on the beach, but I hadn't talked to either of them before this.

Hearing about the giant fossil I found, Miss Elizabeth came to the shop to see it for herself. After examining it carefully, she offered me fifty pounds for it.

It seemed an enormous sum. The blood rushed into my ears and my heart was pounding as I was caught between the desire to say yes, and the knowledge that I could not.

"You've another offer," she guessed when I did not reply at once.

"Not exactly," I stammered. "Squire Henley asked me to promise to save my interesting fossils for him. But I didn't . . ."

"Still, he is your landlord and it would not do to sell it out from under him," she said, understanding my position at once. "There is nothing you can do but wait to see if he is interested. But if he is not, my offer still stands. In the meantime we can study the fossil. With your permission I will do some sketches of it."

Miss Elizabeth came to the shop the very next day carrying a folding stool, pad, pen, ink, and pencils. I watched with fascination as the long, triangular tooth-filled snout, the bony eye with its flower-petallike plates, and the rows of tangled ribs took shape on the paper under her skilled hand. She encouraged me to try sketching it myself. "Keep your eye on the object you are drawing, Mary, not on the paper, but on the fossil itself. That is how the hand learns to copy what the eye sees. Oh now, that is more like it," she said, instructing me. I am grateful to her for the modest skill at drawing fossils that I acquired with her help. It has proved to be very useful to me.

She did several sketches, each from a different angle. While we were sketching, we talked. "Do you think creatures like this are alive now? Not in England, of course, but somewhere else, perhaps?" I asked her.

She looked at me with surprise. "Do you mean to say that you don't think it is a crocodile?"

"I don't know. I have never seen a crocodile," I confessed. "Would a crocodile have legs? This creature doesn't have any."

"Yes, it would, but then I am not the one to ask because I have never seen a crocodile either, only an etching of one," she said, and for some reason we both laughed.

"Do you think it really is a crocodile? Might it be some new creature, one that hasn't been discovered yet?" I asked.

"It may be. That is why I would like to see it made available to comparative anatomists for study."

I didn't know what a comparative anatomist was, and I was too embarrassed to ask. With her keen perception Miss Elizabeth guessed this. "Comparative anatomists are scientists who compare the form of the body of different animals to each other and to fossils to see how they are alike and how they differ. It is the only way we can tell if the creatures we find in fossil form are like those that are living now and how they might be related to one another."

I do not know if it was her admission that she had never seen a crocodile or the easy way she talked to me that made me bold enough to ask a question I had been struggling with myself, but was afraid to ask anyone else, "What if it is not like any living animal? What would that mean?"

The answer she gave was unexpected. "These days, geologists would say that it means the creature no longer exists, that it is extinct."

Extinct? No longer existing? The Reverend Gleed would say that God would not remove entire tribes of his own creation from the earth. "Is it possible that they live somewhere else now or that they have changed over the years?" I asked.

"Some creatures that we find in fossil form have been found alive in other areas of the world, areas with climates that are better suited to them," Miss Philpot said, seeming not to notice my discomfort. "But often there are differences between the fossil and the living creature. And not all the creatures we find in fossil form have been found living. No one has ever found a living ammonite, for example."

I have thought a great deal about this matter, turning it over and over in my mind. I did not want to believe that God would remove entire tribes of animals from the face of the earth. Yet I have found not a few petrified animals and plants that were different from any creatures known to be living now. What happened to them? Did they simply vanish from the earth, become extinct, as Miss Philpot would say? And if they did, how did they vanish? And why? We are told that the ways of God are not easily understood by man. This must be the case with extinction. There must be some purpose, some meaning that we, poor mortals, cannot understand.

The question of extinction leads to another question that has been troubling me. It is written in the Holy Bible that the earth, the seas, the heavens, and everything that dwells therein were created only once "in the beginning." But many of the fossil creatures I find, like the clams and the oysters, though similar to those that live now in the sea, are much, much larger than present-day ones. Some differ in other aspects, as well. How did they come to be different, especially if they were all created at one time?

Whenever I talk about this with Mama, she tells me to read the Bible. She warns me not to be led astray by mere cleverness. I have tried not to stray from God's word, but I have found no answer to my questions in the scriptures. Nothing is written there about ammonites or giant crocodiles with no limbs or about creatures vanishing from the face of the earth. Nor is there anything there that would explain by what process modern-day animals became different from the fossilized ones I find.

As she was packing up her pad and pencils, Miss Philpot invited me to her house on Silver Street that afternoon to look at a new book on geology that had just arrived in the post from Edinburgh. I eagerly ac-

cepted, never stopping to think about the disparity in
our social positions. But when I came to the rambling
house with its many gables, I hesitated. Which entrance
should I knock at? I could call at the trade entrance, but
I had come at the invitation of Miss Philpot. As I stood
there trying to decide, I heard something like a tinkling,
dancing brook, a rushing of sound, more varied than
water, yet somehow cool and refreshing like water. The
music—for I decided that it must be music, though I
had never heard anything like it before—was at once
gay and sad. I was entranced by it, yet it made me
hesitate. I was afraid I would be uncomfortable inside
such a house. Before I could escape, Miss Philpot spied
me through the window.

A girl, about my age, admitted me through the front
door into an entrance hall with a floor of inlaid squares
of wood. Miss Elizabeth Philpot came through a side
door to greet me. Taking me by the hand, she led me
into a large sitting room, the most luxurious I have been
in. I was impressed by the gold-framed mirror which
hung over the carved, painted mantel and by the blue-
flowered carpet that covered the floor. Being the daughter of a cabinetmaker, my eye was caught by the inlaid
mahogany library table set on a single pedestal and by
the lightness and delicacy of the other tables and chairs.

Miss Elizabeth introduced me to her sisters, first the
elder, Miss Mary Philpot, who was seated at the far end
of the room in front of an oblong box on legs that I

later learned was a harpsichord, and then to her younger sister, Miss Margaret Philpot, who was seated on a gold satin damask settee in front of the window with her needlework in her lap. In making these introductions, Miss Elizabeth called me Miss Anning and made much of me, telling her sisters that I was the discoverer of the monster fossil about which all of Lyme was talking.

When we had been introduced, Miss Elizabeth urged me to make myself comfortable, saying that she would fetch the book for me. I sat down beside Miss Margaret, who told me that they were just about to have tea and asked me to join them. I declined out of shyness, but she insisted, saying that I must have been chilled from my walk up the hill.

While we waited for tea to be brought, Miss Mary played the harpsichord. Again there was that rushing of sound, like a brook, that carried me away. Tea was soon brought in by the girl who had admitted me. Her name, I was told, was Betty Beer. She was from Seatown and an orphan. Miss Mary, who left the harpsichord to come sit with us, served us, urging me to take a second helping. When the tea things were cleared away, Miss Elizabeth gave me *The Memoirs of the Wernerian Natural History Society.*

I had never seen a book about geology before. I could scarcely keep myself from opening it and devouring its contents right there. But before I had a chance, Miss Margaret started a conversation, asking with a pleasant smile if she might call me by my Christian name.

"Please do," I told her. I found it strange to be called Miss Anning or even Mary Anning by someone so much older.

"Elizabeth told me that you have some doubts about the identity of the fossil you found. She said that you don't think it is a crocodile?"

"We call it a crocodile," I replied, "because we do not know what else to call it. But somehow, though I have never seen a crocodile, I doubt that this is one."

"Will you be disappointed if it turns out not to be one?" she asked.

Miss Elizabeth answered for me, "Why should she be, Margaret? Whatever it turns out to be will be of interest. After all, the fossil is enormous . . . quite spectacular. It is unlike anything anyone has ever seen before. It is the first entire fossil of its kind that has been found in the world. Crocodile or not, it is causing a stir, and will certainly be of interest to geologists and those who study comparative anatomy."

"If it is not a crocodile, what is it?" Miss Mary asked.

"No doubt it is some creature that is no longer in existence," Miss Elizabeth replied coolly.

But her answer did not seem self-evident to her sister, who said, "I don't know how you can say such a thing, Elizabeth. Just because you have never seen anything like it before does not mean it doesn't exist somewhere on this earth, in other latitudes, perhaps."

* * *

As soon as I returned home I dove into the book that Miss Philpot lent me. From the various memoirs that made up the book, most of which were written by a Mr. Jameson, I understood that Mr. Werner believed that the earth was once covered by a vast sea that periodically receded, leaving portions of the earth bare, and then flooded over it again. The rocks and minerals that make up the surface of the earth have condensed out of the minerals in that sea. It was water, Mr. Werner believed, that shaped the earth as we know it now.

I was taken by this description of the history of the earth because it explained how the fossils of clams, oysters, fish, and other sea creatures that I found in the cliffs had come to be there.

The next day when I told Lizzie that I had been to the Philpot sisters' house on Silver Street, her gray eyes widened with amazement. "Oh, go on! You really went?" she asked.

"Miss Elizabeth Philpot invited me."

"But you needn't have accepted, Mary. You don't belong up on Silver Street," she told me in her knowing way. I did not answer and we continued with our work, I with my fossil preparation and she with her sewing. A few minutes later she looked up from her sewing and asked, "Weren't you uncomfortable?"

"Why should I be? They were very courteous and kind. They made me feel *very* comfortable. They in-

sisted that I stay to tea and that I have second helpings
of everything."

"But Miss Elizabeth Philpot is old. She is at least
thirty, Mary, and not married," Lizzie said. "From the
looks of it, she will never be, poor dear. While she is
not a lady—they say her father is in trade—she is rich.
I shouldn't have liked it."

"But I did like it," I insisted stubbornly. "Miss Elizabeth is interested in fossils and geology. We have things
to talk about. She loaned me a book."

Lizzie shrugged. "I should have known that it was
because of the curiosities," she said. "They are always
leading you into strange places. But come now, tell me
all about it." Which I proceeded to do in some detail.

DISAPPOINTED EXPECTATIONS

 Soon after we brought the crocodile's body up from the beach, I sent another message to Squire Henley informing him that I now had the complete fossil. Still the squire did not come.

Weeks passed and I worked on the fossil, cleaning away some of the Lias in which it was embedded so that it stood out better. The more I worked on the fossil, the more I doubted that it was a crocodile.

My doubts and the squire's failure to appear made me anxious. I had been counting on selling the fossil to him. Had I simply misunderstood him that day when he had jumbled the vertebrae? I so desperately wanted to make money that it was possible that I heard him say what I wished him to say. After all, he was the richest man in the district, and also a collector. What if he did not come? Would I dare sell the fossil to someone else when he was our landlord and he had made me promise to keep it for him? Others besides Miss Philpot had made offers. What if I sold it and then he appeared?

My anxiety was not helped by the advice of our friends and neighbors. Thanks to Mama, they knew of Miss Philpot's offer, and they all had something to say about how I should deal with the squire.

Mr. Littlejohn told me to ask at least sixty-five pounds. "He won't give you that, but if you start high, you'll end up high," he said.

When I went to Mr. Adams to have the chisels sharpened I was told, "You were searching for the body for more a year. The squire should make it worth your while. It is not as if he can buy petrified crocodiles elsewhere."

"Don't let him get away with giving you less because you're a lass," Mrs. Lapham at the market told me when I went to buy cheese. "Let Joseph do the talking for you." She shook her head and corrected herself, "No, he won't do, too young. Your mama should talk for the family. Oh, if only your papa was alive, he would know how to get the most out of Henley. Richard Anning always knew how to deal with the gentry."

Finally, shortly after the new year began, the squire came marching into the shop unannounced. Spying the fossil that was laid out on the workshop floor, he went directly to it and dropped to his knees beside it. "So the talk is true! It really does exist! Amazing!"

He examined the fossil for some time in silence while I looked on anxiously. "I believe this is the fossil that you had in mind, sir. And as I promised, I have saved it for you." He grunted and continued his examination. Anxious, I went on, "But I do not think it is a crocodile."

At this he looked up. "Why do you say that?" he asked.

I explained that its shape wasn't like the picture of a crocodile I had seen in a book. It did not have feet, or at least I could not find them. Also its nostrils were in the wrong position. Then realizing that he might not want it if it was not a crocodile, I added, "But it is a spectacular curiosity, all the same, sir. The biggest I have heard about, seventeen feet when you measure it with all of its vertebrae. You remember, sir, it was the vertebrae that caught your eye that day when you told me that you would buy the creature from me, if ever I found it."

"Yes indeed, it is spectacular. Seventeen feet, you say? It will cause quite a sensation." Then looking at me sharply, he asked, "Where did you say you found this fossil?"

Not understanding the importance of the question, I told him that I found it at the far end of Church Cliffs.

"It was in a piece of the cliff that broke off and fell to the beach, was it not?" he asked.

"Yes, sir," I replied.

I only understood why he was asking these questions a few minutes later when he offered me twenty pounds, saying, "That would be a fair price for the thing, especially since it was in the cliffs on my land to begin with. Generous I should think."

Hearing this figure that was less, much less than I had

hoped for and less than Miss Philpot offered, my face reddened and I was upset, though I tried to remain calm.

Seeing my response, Squire Henley cleared his throat. "No, I think twenty pounds is too little, twenty-three pounds would be a better price."

And twenty-three pounds it was. I could do nothing but accept, since he claimed that it came from his land. I was angry at myself for allowing him to get the better of me, and for allowing myself to get carried away with empty dreams. What a fool I had been!

I heard that Squire Henley bought the crocodile on behalf of Bullock's Egyptian Hall, a giant exhibition hall in Piccadilly Circus in London. People come there to see the wonders of natural history that Mr. Bullock has collected from the South Seas, North and South America, and Africa. My fossil is their most popular exhibit.

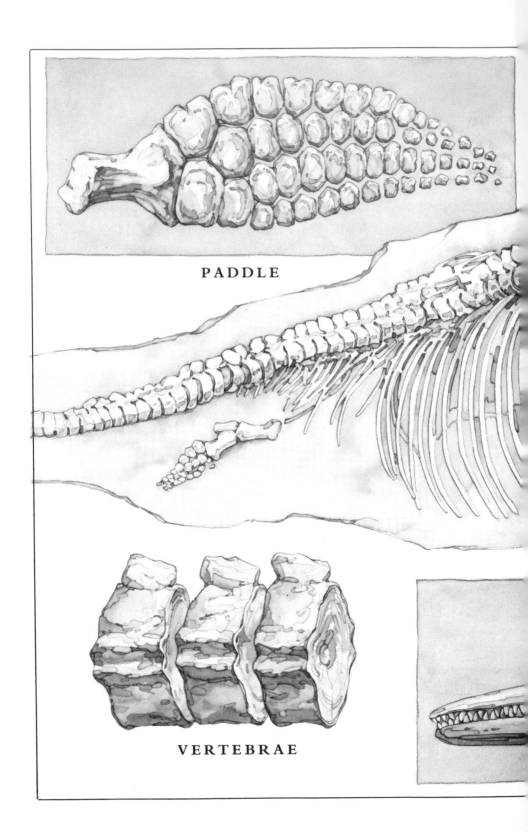

PADDLE

VERTEBRAE

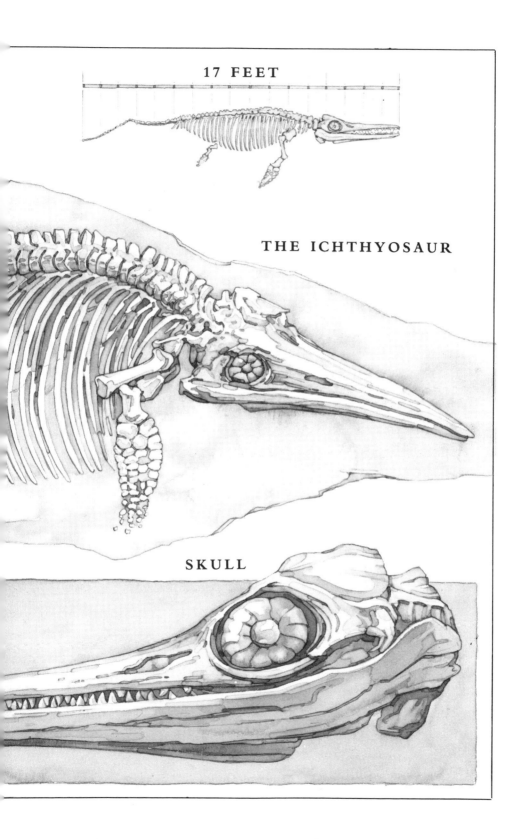

17 FEET

THE ICHTHYOSAUR

SKULL

A CHANCE MEETING

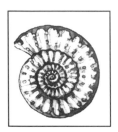Discovering the crocodile had a pro-
found effect on my life. It not only
eased our financial burdens and made
me wonder what had happened to the
animals whose petrified remains I
found, it also led me to become acquainted with a class
of people whom I would not ordinarily know, like the
Philpot sisters. This, in turn, has led to a coolness in my
relations with my neighbors and old acquaintances in
town and a rift between Lizzie and me. But I am getting
ahead of myself now. Painful though it may be, I have
to describe as honestly as I can my meeting with Henry
de la Beche (because my relations with him have cost
me dearly).

Not long after Squire Henley purchased the crocodile, sometime during the spring of 1813, I was working
alone on an isolated ledge in the area of Black Ven when
I had a queer, prickly feeling that someone was watching me. I turned round and started at the sight of a tall,
well-dressed boy, about seventeen years old with sandy-
colored hair, standing behind me. "Hello, Mary," he
said. His deep blue eyes sparkled with merriment.

Who was this strange young master, and why was he

laughing at me, I wondered. I knew he was a gentleman by his clothes—tight-fitting trousers, rather than breeches, a white shirt, and a striped vest, topped by a navy coat. Realizing that I did not remember him, he introduced himself as Henry de la Beche and reminded me that Dr. Carpenter introduced us once when he came to see the crocodile. Then I remembered that he was the young man whom everyone in Lyme was gossiping about. They said he was to come into an income of three thousand pounds a year. A fabulous sum!

He told me that he heard the ring of my hammer when he was down on the beach and climbed up to see who it was. "I've been meaning to call on you for some time. And now, luckily, I've bumped into you here."

"Oh," was all I could think of to say. For a moment there was an awkward silence during which we stood there and looked at one another until it occurred to me to ask why he wanted to see me.

"Geology and fossils," he replied without hesitation. "What else?"

I do not know what it was except perhaps coyness that led me to say, "Oh, there are many other things, sir," but that is what I said. I am embarrassed by it even now!

"Not with you, I am told," he countered. "Your industry and keen eye are the talk of the town. And what I have seen convinces me that what they say is true. I have been standing here for several minutes watching you, and you did not even know I was here."

He smiled at me, shaking his head in wonderment, and suddenly I found myself confessing to this stranger that I often lose myself when I am working. I even told him about being caught by the tide and having to climb the cliffs to escape, a story that I had been ashamed of until that moment. I made much of the danger and hardship, but I did not mention smuggling, or losing my tools.

As I was telling this story, I noticed that he was peering over my shoulder at the cliff where I had been working. When I finished my tale, he asked, "Do you have another crocodile here?"

"Sir, I do not know what it is," I said.

A smile played at the corner of his lips. "You are being mysterious."

"No, not at all, sir," I insisted. "It seems like it might be a bone, but I am not even certain of that." I traced the outline with my chisel for him.

His face grew serious. "I don't know how you saw that it was there. I know I would have walked by and seen nothing. No wonder you found the crocodile." He offered to help me break the fossil out of the cliff.

It was so strange an offer coming from a young gentleman like him that for a moment I thought that he might be having fun at my expense, but before I could think of how to respond, he said, "I am strong even if I am not skilled."

"The cliff is hard and dry, and I was just about to give up," I said.

"You're afraid that I will hurt it," he guessed.

"Oh no, sir. It's not that," I protested. "I really must get back to prepare some curiosities for the shop before the coach arrives tomorrow."

He seemed to be genuinely disappointed, and all of a sudden I felt sorry that I didn't let him help me. "If you are going my way, sir, perhaps we can go back to town together," I suggested.

At this his face became animated. "Perfect! That will give me a chance to pick your brains. You see, I have become fascinated by geology since my return to Lyme," he said. "Dr. Carpenter has been kind enough to let me read his geology books. It was he who suggested that I could learn a great deal from you."

"That is most kind of Dr. Carpenter," I said, "but I'm afraid he might be overestimating how much I know."

"No, you are being too modest. I have heard from others that it would be well worth my while to go fossil hunting with you. I shall pay, of course."

I told him that I do not charge people for coming collecting with me. I like the company. But he insisted that he would pay for whatever we found when we were out together, despite my protestations.

As we made our way down the cliff, scrambling from ledge to ledge, there was one ledge that seemed too far above the next one to descend from. We both hesitated.

Henry jumped first, landing on his feet. He offered me his hand. I was self-conscious about taking it, my hand was so rough and callused. "Take my hand and jump," he urged. "You won't fall. It only looks far."

I reached for his hand, and with my eyes on his face, jumped. I turned my ankle in landing and grimaced in pain. I took a step, trying to act as if nothing had happened. Seeing that I was in pain, Henry insisted that we stop. We sat down on the dirt, and I stretched my leg out in front of me. "I should go fetch some help," he said.

"Please don't," I replied. "It will be fine in a minute."

He suggested that we bind my ankle to lend it support. I protested, but he insisted. Taking a fine, white handkerchief out of his pocket, he folded it into a bandage and, kneeling beside me, wrapped it around my ankle and instep. I was painfully conscious that my stockings were coarse with washing, and that they had been darned many times. "That was clumsy of me. I am glad that you were here," I said.

"If I hadn't been here distracting you, you would not have hurt yourself," he retorted, getting back to his feet. He turned away from me to look out to the bay.

What an awkward mess our meeting had turned into. He must have been sorry that he ever came looking for me. I sat there in miserable silence until my eyes fell on a piece of paper sticking out of his knapsack. Trying to cover the awkwardness of the situation, I asked him what it was. "A sketch of the cliffs," he told me. I asked to see it, saying that I had been learning to sketch fossils.

He took the drawing from his knapsack and unrolled it. It was a rendering of some of the layers of rock in the cliffs along the coast between Lyme Regis and Charmouth. "Do you really think it's good?" he asked, when I told him that I was impressed. Though he smiled, his eyes were serious. "I have been thinking of taking up geology. I like to be out of doors, and I have always been interested in different kinds of rock formations. Now that I am no longer training to be an officer, it seems like a good thing to do." (The gossip in town was that he was dismissed from the Great Marlow military academy for insubordination.)

"Yes, I think it's very good," I said, "but you've already heard that geology and fossils are all I think about."

"Is there anything else worthwhile?" he asked, and we laughed.

"Actually that is why I came to see you," he confessed. "I would like to map the strata of the cliffs around Lyme, and I need to know what fossils are found in each strata."

I didn't know what "strata" were, nor did I know another word he used to describe the rock of the cliffs, "sedimentary," but I guessed at their meaning rather than reveal my ignorance. When I was at home I wrote them down, determined to keep a list of such words and to learn their meanings. My list now fills several pages.

He told me that some geologists believe that fossils are a clue to the comparative ages of the different rocks and their history. Here he was a beginner, yet he was already in touch with the greater world of geology. I was envious and I wanted to impress him with my knowledge. "I can point out things as we walk back," I offered, getting to my feet.

We walked toward town slowly, stopping often as I pointed out where I find different kinds of fossils. My ankle hurt, but I tried not to let it show. By the time we reached the path from the beach, he seemed to have forgotten all about my ankle and ran ahead, expecting me to follow. But the pain made the climb up the steep path difficult for me. When I reached the top, Henry was standing a little way from where the path turns off, chatting with three fashionably dressed girls with short curls around their faces whom I did not know. The way they laughed led me to believe they were friends.

Henry broke away from the group and came toward me. Evidently he had seen me limp because the first thing he said was, "I completely forgot about your ankle. Please forgive me for leaving you behind and rushing ahead." He glanced over to the group of girls. "I have been telling my sister and her friends about my good fortune in finding you out on the cliffs today. They would like to meet you."

Dirty and disheveled as I was from my work, I did

not wish to be introduced to them then and I insisted that I had to get home, saying that I would like to meet them some other time.

We arranged to meet the next day to hunt for fossils. He returned to the group of girls and I continued on my way, careful not to call attention to myself by hobbling. I could hear Henry's voice, probably explaining to the girls why I would not come over to be introduced. Then one of the girls said something I couldn't hear, and they all laughed. It is silly I know, but I felt as if they were laughing at me.

The next morning Mama suggested that I try to stay off my feet. But I had been thinking of nothing else but Henry de la Beche since I left him, remembering every look that passed between us, every smile and word. I wanted to see him again. I told Mama that my ankle did not hurt. But when I could barely walk back from the pump with the pails of water, I was forced to admit that she was right, I was in no condition to go down to the beach. I sent Henry a note telling him that I was unable to meet him.

The morning seemed to drag by as I sat on a stool at the workbench cleaning an ammonite. I stopped every time someone passed by on the street outside, and I waited expectantly, but no one came into the shop.

After waiting this way all morning, I decided that he would not come. Several hours later while I was absorbed in prying away the dried shale that covered the feathery head of a sea lily, I heard a rustle and looked up to see him standing there. He shook his head and smiled broadly, "This is the second time I have come upon you unawares."

"I told you," I said, returning his smile, "I often forget myself when I am working."

He apologized profusely for leaving me behind on the path and insisted that it was because of him that I sprained my ankle. "I was so happy finally to have a chance to talk to you that I forgot myself. I was thoughtless. Will you forgive me?" His eyes held mine for a fraction of a second too long, and I felt my face grow hot.

To change the topic, I asked, "Could I show you some of the fossils I have in the shop?"

"I would like nothing better," he said, "especially if you tell me where you found them so I can mark it on my drawing of the cliffs." He was on his way down to the beach and had the drawing with him.

We cleared the workbench and spread the sketch out on it, weighing its corners down with fossils. I got up to fetch a fossil to show him, but when he saw me hobble, he suggested that he bring them to me while I sat. "You don't know where anything is," I objected. But he would have it no other way, and I gave in.

He brought me almost everything I had in the shop to identify, including a large crocodile vertebrae.

"I don't think the creature was actually a crocodile," I explained, picking up the vertebrae from the table. "We only call the fossil that because we do not know what else to call it. Miss Philpot says that it should be given to a comparative anatomist who can determine what it was, but I don't think it will be. Squire Henley bought it for a London museum."

"I shall buy the next fossil like that you find and make it available for study," he said.

His easy assumption that there would be another one and that I would sell it to him irritated me. "First it has to be found," I retorted.

He held up another vertebrae, seeming not to notice the edge in my voice. "Well, it seems as if you are working on another one," he said.

"No, it is not the same. At first glance it seems to be, but if you look closely you will see there are differences." I had him bring me a vertebrae like the ones from Henley's crocodile, and with the two side by side I pointed out the differences.

He suggested that it might be another type of crocodile. I was immediately jealous that it was he who had thought of that possibility and not I. "We need to have more of it to tell," I said.

"Maybe I could help you find more," he offered eagerly.

"It's not mine to find," I replied. "Anyone can go out there and look."

"Oh, I didn't mean it that way. I only meant that I could help you search for it, if you would permit me to, that is," he apologized. "It would be thrilling to bring to light something that has been entombed so long. How long ago do you think the creature lived?"

It was something I had been wondering about but had never discussed with anyone before because I was afraid my questions would be dismissed.

"Sometime long, long ago . . . in distant ages," I said.

"Do you think it was before man?"

"I don't know, but I haven't found any fossilized human bones or traces of man in the rocks. But the Bible says—"

He interrupted me, "You don't believe that God created the heavens and earth and all that lives in six days, do you?" His eyes challenged me.

I pulled back, shocked by his question. "I believe in the Bible and its truth," I said.

"Do you believe the biblical description of the creation is a scientific account?" he asked.

I turned away. "I don't know about science," I confessed.

He was not satisfied by my admission of a doubt that was causing me so much pain (and still does), and he continued to press me until I said, "How could it be possible? The days that the Bible speaks of could not be days as we know them now. It seems too short a time. But maybe . . . I just don't know."

Henry nodded his head sympathetically, but did not say anything except, "Yes . . . yes . . ." The topic was dropped without my ever learning what he believed, though it was evident that he doubted the literal truth of the biblical description.

He resumed fetching me fossils to identify for him, bringing me two bits of fossil skull and a few vertebrae that I had put away in a far corner of the workshop. They were different from anything else I had found. Seeing them, I said, "Oh, those. I have no idea what creature they are from or even if all of those bits are from the same creature."

"You have them in the same place so you must think these are from the same creature."

"They are in the same place because I found the pieces all jumbled up together over in the ledges of Black Ven. But it's possible that they aren't all from the same animal."

"You certainly are mysterious when it comes to your finds," he said, laughing.

"I am not being mysterious," I insisted. "I just don't know what to say about them because I don't know what the creature looked like or what it was, except that if these bits are all from the same creature, it had a small head," I said, showing him the curve of the skull. "See how small it is. But I have no idea what the rest of the creature looks like."

"Maybe it looks like this," he said, picking up his pen

and quickly sketching a funny-looking, small-headed, large-bodied creature with long ears, a pointed tail, and a scaly body on a piece of paper. Then he sketched another with a tiny head and long sloping body.

"My turn," I said, taking the pen and sketching an odd-looking creature. We continued in this way taking turns, drawing each creature more fantastic than the last, until I reached for the pen and knocked his hand into the bottle and splashed ink all over his drawing of the cliffs. We both jumped up in horror and immediately tried to repair the damage. I found some rags that I used to wrap the curiosities in and blotted up as much of the ink as I could, but the drawing was ruined. "It was not very good," Henry said, "just a beginning." A few minutes later he mumbled something about it being late, and left.

A STOLEN FOSSIL

 After spilling the ink, I was deeply embarrassed. I had allowed myself to become too familiar too quickly. I had been carried away by the pleasure of having someone to talk to about the fossils, and then I had ruined his drawing. I was certain he would never want to see me again. I thought I would die with shame if I saw him again. Yet I found myself lingering as I walked past the tall windows of his house on Broad Street, hoping that he would look out and see me. I did not see him there, nor did I see him on the beach, or in town. I was disappointed and, at the same time, relieved.

Much to my surprise a few weeks later a freckle-faced lad in footman's livery came by the shop with a note on a white pasteboard card from Henry, asking after my ankle. I read the few lines over several times searching for some hidden meaning and finally decided there was none; it was a polite note, nothing more. There was no reason for me not to answer. I scribbled a reply, sending it back by the same messenger. In no time at all, the lad was back with a second note from Henry asking if I would be willing to take him out collecting that afternoon. I did not know what I should do. I was afraid things would get out of hand again, and I would embarrass myself. At the same time I wanted very much to go. I promised myself that if I went, I would be businesslike and not let myself be carried away. If I were proper and reserved, he would be, too. (It was not until later that I discovered many people in Lyme considered it improper for me to take young gentlemen out fossil hunting under any circumstances.) I wrote back telling him to meet me at the shop when the clock at the marketplace was at two.

Despite my resolve to behave in a businesslike way I could not bring myself to put on my old, dark apron. I put on my new, white one. I stepped outside to look at the clock. It was only a few minutes after eleven. I tried to work on the fossils, but I was too impatient and I broke an urchin. After dinner, I cleared away the dishes. I brushed my hair and put on my bonnet, the straw with blue underside and ribbons to match, and not the battered hat that I usually wore.

Seeing me, Mama asked, "Are you going visiting?" I confessed that I was going collecting. "In your Sunday bonnet and new apron?" she asked.

Before I could think of how to answer her, Joseph, who had stopped by on his way to the marketplace, said, "She's preening for the young master."

"No, I am not," I said between clenched teeth, rushing at him.

Chanting, "Mary's preening for the young master," he darted out of reach. I chased him round the table. The bell on the shop door rang, and I escaped down the stairs. It was Henry. I grabbed my bag of tools, and we were out the door and into the street.

Henry's manner was as natural and easy as if nothing had happened. He had been in Bristol on business with his stepfather, Mr. Aveline. "I have never been out of Lyme," I said enviously. We made our way up the narrow lane past the baths and down Long Entry to the beach path. "But someday, someday soon I will go to London to see the sights and visit my crocodile at Bullock's in Piccadilly Circus."

"I hope you are not disappointed by London," Henry said, smiling at me kindly. He was born in London and has been there many times. He had even been to Jamaica, where he owns sugar plantations and slaves.

We scrambled down the path with growing excitement. On reaching the level of the beach, Henry threw out his arms, exclaiming, "We are going to find great things today, Mary. Crocodiles, elephants, who knows what?"

"Something big and spectacular," I said, entering his mood, and we both laughed.

He touched my sleeve, "I know what we should look for—the creature with the small head. I want to see what it really looked like."

Embarrassed by the reminder of our last meeting, I

said, "No, not that." He did not reply and we were both quiet for a minute as we walked along. Then, feeling bad that I had rejected his plan, I said, "Let's look for another petrified crocodile. We need another to find out what it really was."

"Well, tell me," he asked, still jesting, "how does one find a petrified crocodile?"

I became serious. "By keeping a sharp eye out." I instructed him, much as Papa instructed me, as we walked along the beach. "Be patient and look, really look, at the face of the cliffs, especially where the cliff face has broken away and the bare rock is exposed. There is a lot of looking to be done before you see fossils and especially before you try to remove them."

As we passed Church Cliff, I pointed out some fossils. "Why aren't we stopping to collect them?" he asked. I explained that they most likely were gryphea—oysters —and I already had enough of them. He asked me how I knew. "I am guessing that it's an oyster because of the bed it's in. Strata, you called it," I said, using the word for the first time.

"Oh, I should have known that," he said, laughing good-naturedly at himself.

I suggested that we go to Black Ven. "Do you think that we shall find a crocodile there?" he asked.

"It is more likely that we'll find ammonites, but you never know for certain," I said, and we both laughed at the possibility. I felt strangely happy, sad, and restless.

I felt like flying, but instead I started to run. Henry ran after me. I slid on the slippery seaweed-draped pebbles, recovered my balance, and ran on.

Henry was not so fortunate. Flapping his arms like a giant bird, he fell so that he was sitting on the wet seaweed with his legs stretched out in front of him. He looked so surprised that I could not help laughing at him, even though I knew it was cruel. He laughed, too, picked himself up, brushed off his trousers, and we ran on along the shore toward Black Ven. After we rounded the headland, we scrambled up the ledges, stopping to catch our breath from time to time. I pointed out a particularly fossil-rich bed. We stopped when we reached the ledge where he found me that day we met. I went off in search of the chisel mark I had made in the rock. While I was looking for it, I saw something else that caught my eye. I put down my bag and took out my chisel and hammer. Henry called to me, saying that he found the chisel mark. "I have something more important," I shouted.

"If it is a crocodile, wait for me," he shouted back.

"I don't know what it is," I said, pointing out the bone-white streak in the ledge to him as he rushed up.

"But you do believe it belongs to a crocodile?" he asked.

"Too early to tell," I cautioned. "We won't know what we have until we have some of the surrounding stone cleared away." We set to work immediately. We

soon found that the marl in which the fossil was embedded was hard and that we could make little progress
with the tools we had. Henry offered to go back and
fetch some heavier tools and a workman so that we
could continue, but I pointed out that it was growing
dark and that the tide had turned. He reluctantly agreed
to wait for low tide the next day. After trying to work
with the tools that we had for a while longer, we
stopped.

The sun was low and the tide was coming in quickly
when we reached the beach. We had only a narrow path
left between the cliffs and the incoming waves. Near
Church Cliff we were caught by a wave. When I saw
him spluttering and soaked in his fine clothes, I burst out
laughing. He pointed and laughed at me, and I realized
that I must look ridiculous, too, wearing my Sunday
bonnet with my clothes wet through to the skin.

I caught Henry's eye as we started up the path from
the beach, and we both laughed again.

As we walked from Long Entry lane onto the Butter-
market we passed Mr. Clerkenwell, who stopped in his
tracks to turn and stare at the two of us in our wet
clothes. His shocked look only added to our hilarity.

It rained during the night, the first rain in weeks. It was
a steady downpour that fell all night and into the morning. Water ran in rivulets down the streets and alleys
of Lyme into the river and from there out to sea with

a rushing, roaring sound. As if by plan, the rain stopped by midmorning. The sun broke through, sparkling off the sea and off the windowpanes in town, dazzling the day itself with its bright rays. Fool that I was, I believed that nature herself was on our side.

I gathered my tools as soon as we finished dinner. Mama asked me to run to the egg woman to buy some eggs and cheese for supper. "Mr. de la Beche will be here with the workmen at two-thirty," I protested.

"It shan't take you but a few minutes. Besides, you should not go out so soon after a rain. It isn't safe," Mama said, sending me off. But I was so eager to go that I dismissed her warning.

I ran to the marketplace, darting in and out of the crowd from the surrounding countryside buying and selling their produce and animals, trying not to bump into anyone. I looked up at the clock on the steeple and my heart sank. It was nearly three o'clock. I was late and I was going to keep him waiting. I ran all the way home with the eggs and the cheese. I burst into the shop breathlessly and ran up the stairs to our rooms. Henry was not there.

I took off my bonnet and brushed my hair again. Then I went downstairs. I looked at the tools I had in my sack, taking them out and putting them back in: a mallet, two geological hammers—one heavier than the other—a few cold chisels, a brush, some dropcloths. I picked up a broom and swept the shop. When I finished,

I tidied the workbench. The chimes of St. Michael's rang three-thirty.

"I have had a deuce of time finding someone to work for us," he explained when he arrived soon afterward. "They all said that it was foolhardy to go to Black Ven after a rain. Jim Greengrass here is the only one who would agree to come." About thirteen or fourteen years old, Jim Greengrass had a thatch of black hair and eyes that were small, black currants in his pudding of a face. Henry found him at the market where he had come to look for a day's work.

"They may be right," I admitted reluctantly. "There are more likely to be slides after a rain. Perhaps we should not go."

"I am going no matter what," Henry said. "I've thought of nothing else, and I'm not waiting another day. Anyway, the rain will make the digging easier, won't it?"

I admitted that it would. Caught up in Henry's enthusiasm, I made light of the danger and, turning to Jim Greengrass, asked, "Are you afraid?"

He looked down at his dirty, bare feet. "He's paying me good money," Jim said in a hoarse whisper, indicating Henry with a nod of his chin, "and I need the work. I'll take my chances." We agreed on going.

The three of us made good progress at breaking the fossil out. By the time the sun set we could see that we had a jawbone, perhaps more, but we could not tell without several hours of work. It was growing dark as we began to make our way down the ledges to the beach. At one point the moon, which had been lighting our way, was covered by clouds and we could not see anything. Jim Greengrass, afraid of misstepping and falling, sat down on the ledge and refused to go farther. There was nothing for Henry and me to do but to sit down, too. Jim Greengrass did not talk, but Henry and I, who were excited by our find, were making plans for extracting it. In the midst of our conversation, there was a rumble from deep in the earth. We froze, not knowing what to do. There was a deafening roar as the earth only a few feet from where we were sitting split off from the cliff and broke apart. We watched in horror as it fell and crashed to the beach below and kept falling, pouring, tumbling from the cliff in a wild, rushing river of rocks, dirt, and bushes. Gradually, the falling rocks and dirt tapered off so that only a trickle of dirt fell, and then it stopped altogether. It was quiet once more, except for the pounding of my heart, which was as deafening to me as the slide itself. Some time passed before we dared speak and when we did, we whispered as if the earth itself might hear us and begin to roar again.

In the quiet aftermath I heard Jim Greengrass mumble to himself, "They're mad, mad to come here. I could have been killed for an old jawbone!"

After what seemed like an eternity of waiting, the

moon appeared again, giving us a shadowy light to see our way by. Subdued and quiet, we scrambled down to the beach and made our way back to town. The tide was almost in, but we were afraid to stay too close to the cliffs and were forced out into the surf. We were wet through by the time we reached town.

Except for an occasional lamp flickering from an uncurtained window, the streets of Lyme were dark. We parted in front of the shop with whispered promises to meet the next afternoon.

To say that Mama was worried when I was late and that her worry turned to anger when she learned that I was safe, is to make brief what was in actuality a tiresome scene in which I was subjected to a tirade about my reckless behavior. Why did I go to Black Ven so soon after a storm? Didn't I know that it is dangerous? Was it because of Henry de la Beche that I went? Was I so smitten by his charms that I had taken leave of my senses, even staying out after dark with him? She could see that I was not the same girl since I had met him. "Preening, standing in front of the glass, wearing your Sunday bonnet to go collecting. And those looks you give each other. Don't think that I am blind to such things. You are being foolish, Mary. He has a fortune, and he is not our kind. He is just amusing himself with you and your fossils because he has nothing better to do now. He'll drop you as soon as something else comes along."

I lowered my head and let Mama's scolding wash over me. I did not dare say anything in my own defense. When she was done, I apologized for causing her to worry. I knew she was right, that it was foolish to have gone. I should not have allowed myself to be swayed by Henry's enthusiasm, knowing that it was dangerous.

But I would not admit the rightness of anything else that she said. She was treating me as if I were still a child. But I was no longer a child. I was fourteen. She attacked me for standing in front of the glass, but I did not see anything wrong with that. Why should I not try to be pleasing to others? I am not unpleasant looking, even though I am not pretty in the soft way Lizzie is. My hair is dark and glossy, and people say my eyes, which are my best feature, are intelligent.

Her comment about the looks Henry and I gave each other made me especially furious because I was embarrassed by it and did not want to admit that there was anything special between us. Instead, I told myself that Henry and I understood one another because we were both interested in fossils and geology. But what did Mama know? Nothing! Nothing about my interests in fossils or geology. The fossils were no more than a way to make money as far as she was concerned. She did not want to know what they were or why they were there or anything else about them, except what they would fetch. And her statement about Henry amusing himself with me and the fossils was unfair. What did she know about that? She had never spoken to him. She knew nothing about him, except the town gossip. I knew that his interest in geology was a serious one. Dr. Carpenter must have thought so, too. Why else would he spend time with him and encourage him?

Mama's tirade made me angry and defiant. I decided to meet Henry just as we planned. Mama did not expressly forbid it. But I promised myself that I would be careful not to give her cause for worry.

It was not Mama who stopped us from meeting Saturday morning, but the weather. It began to rain during the night and continued all day, making it impossible to go out. It did not clear until late Sunday. Chastened by our last experience after a rain, we decided to wait a few days. We set out on Thursday morning at dawn as the tide was starting out. Jim Greengrass, who had promised that he and one of his brothers would meet us on the beach, was not there. After waiting for them for some time, Henry suggested that we go on without them. "I have been shut in the house, thinking about getting my hands on the fossil for days now and they shall not stop me. We can always go back to town and get someone to come out with a litter when we are ready," he said.

Henry ran on ahead as we approached the site. I was still climbing when I heard him yell, "Mary! Mary, come here!" His voice sounded at once surprised and outraged. I arrived to find him looking in dismay at a hole. There was a mound of dirt and rock surrounding the hole. "It's been taken. The fossil is gone," Henry said.

"Taken? Who would do such a thing?" I asked, unable to believe what I saw.

"A lot of people." Henry shook his head sadly. "Everyone in town dreams of finding a crocodile, now that you have found one and sold it to Squire Henley."

I had been so caught up in being the one who found the crocodile that I had only been dimly aware of others' jealousy, but now that Henry had put it into words, I knew it was true. Still I could not bring myself to believe that someone would actually steal one of my finds. "Do you think someone just happened to come upon it?"

Henry smiled sadly. "It's not likely, Mary. This is not the place for a casual stroll. It must have been someone who knew about it, who knew where it was, and who came here deliberately to take it."

"Jim Greengrass," we said in unison. He was the only one who knew where we were working. But still I didn't want to believe it. "We can't be sure it was Jim Greengrass. He was scared Friday. It doesn't seem likely that he would come back here. It might have been someone else. Who else knew about it?" I asked.

"Everyone. I was so proud, I told everyone who would listen that I found part of a crocodile in Black Ven," Henry admitted.

We did not talk much on the way back to town. Nevertheless, when we reached the shop, we did not go our separate ways immediately. We stood outside for some time going over and over everyone who might possibly have taken our find, coming back to Jim Greengrass every time. My heart felt heavy and I wanted to cry, but I couldn't. "It doesn't matter who took it, there is nothing we can do about it. Anyone who wants to can take my finds, and there is no way I can stop them. But if it keeps happening, I shall have to find some other line of work," I said to Henry.

"You cannot let someone take your finds that way," Henry said. "It is yours. You found it. They wouldn't have known where it was if you hadn't. And we uncovered it. Whoever took it is a thief. They must be stopped."

Mrs. Cruikshanks passed by on her way to market, and I was conscious of how we must look to the neighbors standing there talking so long. I broke off our conversation.

"I shall find out who did it, and I shall make them very sorry," Henry called to me as I stepped in the doorway.

Lyme being such a small place, word of the theft got around quickly. At the smith's that afternoon, Robert Cruikshanks, who was sharpening my chisels, said something about a fossil, which I couldn't hear over the noise of the metal clanging. "What did you say?" I shouted.

Stopping the hammer in midair, Robert cocked his head to one side so that he was looking up at me with one large brown eye like a bird, "Said I heard someone picked off the young gentleman's crocodile." He was chuckling to himself as he brought the hammer down on the chisel, sending sparks flying.

"Who told you that?" I demanded.

"Word gets round," he said, bending over to plunge the chisel into a bucket of cold water.

"It was I who found that crocodile, and I say that whoever took it is a thief."

He straightened and his eyes met mine. "It was still in the cliff, was it not? There for the taking. It's not yours until you have it off the beach."

"He's a thief all the same," I countered angrily.

"Well, thief or not, someone else has it and will make a pretty penny off it, and there is not a thing you or the young gentleman can do about it." Chuckling to himself, he turned his back to me and pulled the chisel out of the water.

Robert Cruikshanks thought it was amusing that someone took my find. I knew that he had never been my friend, but he was my neighbor. Why would he wish me ill? He never had before. He seemed pleased enough for me when I found the crocodile and he was angry on my behalf when Henley paid me so little. Why was he glad now? What had I done to offend him? Had I been too proud? I went over and over my conduct to see if I had given him or anyone else cause for offense. But I could not think of any reason why they should be angry with me. That they were jealous of my good fortune in finding the crocodile and selling it to Squire Henley I was willing to believe, but that did not seem to be sufficient cause for such maliciousness.

JOSEPH TAKES MATTERS INTO
HIS OWN HANDS

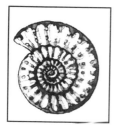 Joseph stopped by the shop later in the day to tell me that everyone in the marketplace was talking about the theft. "They said someone pinched de la Beche's crocodile."

"De la Beche's fossil?" I said, beginning to understand why Robert Cruikshanks found the theft amusing. He thought Jim Greengrass stole it from de la Beche, and that de la Beche's finds were fair game because he was already rich. "It was my find," I told Joseph. "Mr. de la Beche would have paid me for it."

"Everyone says it was de la Beche's," he said.

"It was mine," I repeated, explaining that I found the fossil, and that my agreement with Henry was that he bought whatever of value either of us found when we were out collecting together.

Joseph was upset by this intelligence. The story of the theft was amusing when it was de la Beche's fossil, but now that he saw that I was the loser, he was angry. "We cannot let Jim Greengrass get away with it," he said heatedly. "I shall give him a thrashing, one he'll remember the rest of his life."

"Please leave well enough alone," I told him. I felt

hopeless and sad, sensing that behind people's amusement at the theft of Henry's fossil by a poor laborer lay resentment at his wealth and disapproval of my connection with him. I could see that if Joseph fought with Jim Greengrass it would only make matters worse.

"Then he and everyone else will think that they can pick off your finds anytime they choose. We cannot let it be. I must teach him a lesson and when I do, I am going to see that word of it gets round town. I want everyone to know that if anyone touches your finds again they will have to face me."

It happened a week or two later. Mama and I had finished supper, cleared away the dishes, and were sitting around the table. I was reading to Mama from *Pilgrim's Progress* when Joseph burst into the house. His cheek was bruised, his lip swollen, and his shirt bloody. Alarmed by his appearance, Mama and I rushed to do what we could to minister to his wounds. Brushing our efforts aside, he launched into an excited account of his fight with Jim Greengrass.

This is what I remember of it.

Not wanting to attack Jim Greengrass in the marketplace where others might come to his aid, Joseph and Robert Whitesides lured him to the Cobb at sunset with the promise of a keg, which they said they had uncovered on the beach and wanted him to sell for them.

Suspecting nothing, Jim Greengrass came by himself. As he approached the meeting place, Joseph jumped out and fell upon him, knocking him down on the stones. He rolled, trying to throw Joseph off, but Joseph held fast, clinging to him with one arm round his neck and beating him on the head with the other.

In the midst of the struggle Jim Greengrass threw Joseph off, got to his feet, and ran. In his confusion, he ran to the far end of the Cobb. Joseph was soon after him in pursuit. When Jim saw that he was at the end of the wall and could go no further, he realized that he was caught, but before he could make a dash for it, Joseph was on him. Jim swung at Joseph. Joseph ducked his punch and kicked him. Jim fell to the pavement. Joseph pinned Jim to the stones to keep him from rolling over the edge of the wall into the sea. Then he took Jim by the shoulders and threatened to throw him over if he didn't tell him what he did with the fossil. At first Jim wouldn't say. But when Joseph started to drag him as if he really meant it, Jim began to talk. He admitted that he had sold the fossil. But when Joseph demanded to know who bought it, all Jim would tell him was that it was a man from Charmouth.

"Oh, Joseph, you were hurt, and it was because of me. You shouldn't have!" I exclaimed when Joseph finished his story.

Mama shook her head disapprovingly. "Now look at you, Joseph," she said. "Look at you. What did you do with that fighting? You didn't get the fossil, did you, son? But you did get bruised and bloody. This shan't be the end of it, I tell you. It'll be a wonder if Jim Green-grass doesn't come back to town with some of his brothers to give you a beating in return for the one you gave him. And what for? You are a poor boy, and so is he. Poor boys fighting over a few petrified bones because the rich will pay for them, and all of Lyme laughing over it. You should have left well enough alone."

Surprised by our response, Joseph repeated, "I gave Jim Greengrass such a scare he won't steal any of our fossils again. Nor will anyone else when they hear."

"When they hear? If you've a brain in your head, Joseph, you'll keep your mouth shut so people won't hear unless you want more trouble," Mama warned him.

Poor, poor Joseph! How confusing it all must have been for him. Being straightforward and loyal, he understood that a wrong had been done and he wished to right it. Not understanding anything else about the situation, he expected us to be grateful and to treat him like a hero. Instead, what he got for all his trouble were some cuts and bruises and a scolding from Mama. Not even I, whose honor he was defending, could be glad for what he had done, though I felt sorry for him and loved him deeply for having done it.

THE END OF A FRIENDSHIP

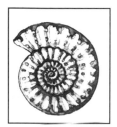

Lizzie came to visit the next morning. She sat on Papa's stool and sewed, as she often did when she dropped by, while I worked on the fossils. I was telling her about what happened on the Cobb, and said, "I wish Joseph hadn't taken matters into his own hands like that—it will just cause more trouble. And I don't think it will stop anyone from taking my fossils, especially now that Jim Greengrass has sold it. He sold it to someone in Charmouth, admitted as much to Joseph. But he doesn't know his name."

Lizzie looked up from her work. "Your fossil? I thought it was Henry de la Beche's."

"No, it was mine, Lizzie. I found it, Henry was to have paid me for it."

"Jim Greengrass stole the curiosity from de la Beche," Lizzie said. "That's what everyone is saying."

"So then it's fine, just fine to take it. Is that what they say?" I asked heatedly.

"No, not exactly, Mary. It didn't belong to Jim Greengrass. But he didn't know he was taking it from you. He thought he was taking it from that rich young dandy."

"Henry de la Beche was with me. I was taking him out, showing him."

Lizzie fastened her gray eyes on me. "You and him. Everyone is talking about the two of you. Everyone, Mary. I try to defend you. I tell them that Mr. de la Beche is interested in geology and that you are showing him where you find curiosities. But no one believes me. My own mother called me a fool when I told her that."

My face was burning, and Lizzie saw it. She said, "I'm only telling you this because we are friends. It is for your own good, Mary. People think it's not right for you to be alone with him."

"Alone? Lizzie, I am not alone with him. I am out on the beach where everyone in the world can see us. Sometimes we are out at Black Ven, but anyone who likes can come there. I am teaching him where to find curiosities, and he is paying me for what we find. I don't understand what they are talking about. Some people just don't like my hunting curiosities. And they are jealous of my finding the crocodile."

"All I am saying, Mary, is people do not think it is proper for you to be out there with him. They think that young Mr. de la Beche is taking advantage of you, and if he hasn't yet, he will soon enough."

I managed a forced, hollow laugh.

Lizzie's gray eyes glinted like steel. "It is not a laughing matter, Mary. You have always thought you were better than us, even when you were in chapel school.

But finding petrified monsters that the gentry pay for does not excuse you from behaving properly or put you above the censure of your friends and neighbors. You are still one of us. You are still subject to the same standards of conduct."

"Small, narrow standards enforced by slander and gossip," I replied bitterly, trying to keep my voice down so that Mama did not hear.

"Slander? Come now, Mary. Is there not something else going on besides collecting between you and Henry de la Beche? I have seen you and de la Beche. I have seen the way you look at him, and I am not the only one who has. That is why they are gossiping. All I am saying, Mary, is watch yourself, if you do not want to be the object of scorn!" She gathered up her sewing, got off the stool, and left, while I stood by not knowing what to say to stop her.

Too late I called out to her, "Oh, Lizzie, don't *you* think badly of me." But she had closed the door behind her and could not hear me.

HOPES, DREAMS, AND A LONELY REALITY

 Lizzie's words ring in my ears to this day. Who can be insensitive to such accusations? I tried to avoid Henry de la Beche. I did not go fossil hunting with him. I made polite excuses so that he did not suspect anything. I dreaded meeting him somewhere on the beach or in town and having to explain myself to him because I was afraid that I would lose my resolve, which is exactly what happened.

One morning on my way to buy provisions for the house I stopped to join the crowd watching a group of acrobats on the edge of the marketplace. I was applauding one of the troop who had just done a backward somersault over the bodies of four volunteers, when I heard a voice in my ear, "Hello, Mary." I turned round and there was Henry. My heart leapt. I could not be unfriendly, I was too happy to see him. We talked for minute or two, and before I knew it, we had made arrangements to meet at the far end of Monmouth Beach when the tide turned later that day. It is a secluded place where we were unlikely to be seen by others.

He must have known, had he given it any thought,

that I was putting my reputation at risk by meeting him on the beach. But perhaps he did not know how serious the consequences were for me, not at first. He knew little about Lyme and could not imagine how gossip is used as a weapon here.

I met him that day and many times after that—all through the summer and into the autumn— taking care each time that we were not seen by people who would talk. I met him, knowing that others disapproved and that my reputation was being harmed, because I could not bear to stay away. I lived for those meetings, thirsting for them as a plant thirsts for water.

If anyone were to spy on us while we were out together they would have been most disappointed. Our behavior gave little cause for disapproval (except for the disapproval that was already attendant on our meeting and on the fact that I was engaged in such an "unfeminine" pursuit as curiosity collecting). It was only my thoughts that were scandalous. Lying in my bed at night, I sometimes imagined Henry taking me in his arms and gazing longingly into my eyes and making passionate vows of love to me. But in actuality, he never did. When we were together we talked not about love, but about geology—fossils, strata, crocodiles, and small-headed creatures. We did not embrace or kiss, we looked for fossils together, finding among other things a fossil brittle starfish in good condition, a couple of fish, (hybodus and dapedium) a new kind of ammonite, and a few fossil bones of the crocodile.

For Henry I was little more than a guide to fossils. That may be harsh, but I must face it. It was I who dreamt of him. There was no sign that he dreamt of me. That is not to say that he did not like me. There were a few times when he almost said something personal, but he quickly caught himself and turned the situation round with a joke so that we were soon laughing. It is Henry's way to poke fun and tease when things are in danger of becoming serious.

That is why I found it strange when, one day, as we were walking west along the shore toward Pinhay Bay talking about sea lilies that we hoped to find there, he said without warning, "You know, Mary, you are the only person I can talk to honestly. I am always pretending with others, always talking about things I am not interested in. It is only with you that I can be my real self."

I blushed and looked away so that he would not see. My heart was pounding, and I did not know what to say. But he did not seem to notice. "My family is treating me as if I still am a willful, ungovernable boy. They think my passion for geology is misguided and will pass. They planned on my being in the army and were disappointed when I left Great Marlow. They have no idea what to do with me now. They are insisting that I come with them to London."

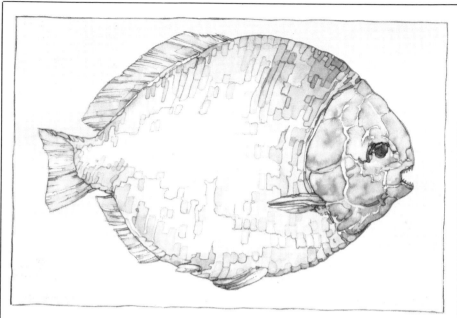

DAPEDIUM

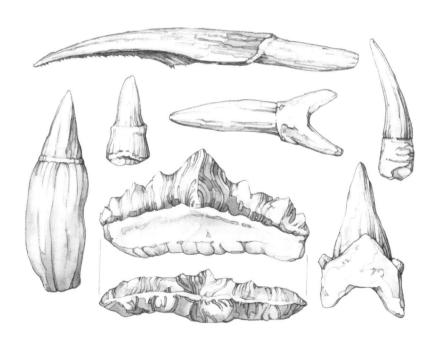

FOSSILIZED TEETH AND SCALES

With a sinking feeling, I understood that he was being sent away, away from me.

"I tried to convince my mother to stay, or even to leave me behind here in Lyme, but she would not hear of it. I must go, and that is all there is for it." His voice rose as he said this as if he were trying to convince me.

I was not convinced. How could he leave in autumn, the best time for collecting? How could he leave me? Mama and Lizzie said that he was just using me to pass the time while he was in Lyme. I had to admit that they might be right. Soon he would be in London, and he would not give me, the fossils, or Lyme another thought. A sea gull called. It sounded like a cry.

"When are you leaving?" I asked, turning back to look at him.

"Tomorrow," he replied.

My eyes met his for a second, and then I turned away again. I did not want to be there with him. It was as if by saying that he was leaving, he had already gone and left me behind. And if I was not with him, I did not know why I was there at all. After a while, I made some excuse and started for home.

I had not walked far, when he caught up with me. "I shall be back for Christmas," he said, falling in step beside me.

"That will be nice," I replied, afraid to say more.

Not seeming to notice my emotion, he said, "In the meantime, please keep me informed of your finds. I was looking forward to winter and its storms and to fossil hunting with you then. You know, Mary, I still have crocodile fever, and I still plan to discover what the beast was. Going to London is only a distraction . . . but one I must give in to now. They will see soon enough that I am passionate about geology and will leave me to pursue it."

My heart eased. He was being forced to leave against his will. His family insisted that he go. Then I despaired again as it became apparent to me that even if this was the case, our friendship was doomed. His mother insisted that he go because she had heard the town gossip. She was afraid that he had become involved with a village girl from the laboring class, a cabinetmaker's daughter, an inappropriate choice for a young man with a fortune. She was trying to get him away from me and from the fossils. She thought that London with its amusements, society, and eligible young ladies would distract him, and he would forget about geology and fossils, and that he would lose interest in me.

We parted on the beach far from town as had become our custom. I walked back along the beach to Lyme by myself.

I did not mention Henry's departure to Mama. Believing that I no longer was meeting him down on the beach when I went fossil hunting, she did not realize that things had changed. I still went down to the beach to hunt fossils, still cleaned and prepared them in the workshop, and I still sold them to the travelers, though there were few travelers at that time of year. These were the things that had occupied me before. But after Henry left I was lonely. I missed our meetings on the beach, the excitement of finding things together, talking about them, wondering what they were as we worked to break them out of the rock. More than anything I missed the laughter.

In the past I had always confided in Lizzie. We talked about everything and nothing—other girls, dresses that we wanted, clothes that we had seen, the behavior of the boys in chapel, how her sister Catherine was being visited by a certain young man from Axe with refined manners who was a journeyman smith, the Reverend Gleed's sermon, the peculiar way that Mrs. Hale had of snorting like a horse when she disapproved of something, how Mrs. Gleed managed to wheedle her way into people's confidence so that she knew everyone's secrets. We wondered together about the state of our souls and whether we would find favor in God's eyes. Now she, too, had gone from me. She had not stopped by the shop since that day she had warned me about Henry. When we met, she still greeted me, but it was not the same. She did not ask me to stop by her house, nor did she invite me to sit with her at meeting. And if she did, would I have gone? Perhaps. But I knew that it would not be the same. I could no longer tell her what I was thinking about or doing. My friendship with

Henry and my growing interest in fossils had made us distant. I had no one my own age to talk to, and I was lonely.

As Christmas drew near I found myself thinking about Henry. I expected him to return to Lyme for the holidays. Would he come by the shop? Perhaps he was no longer interested in geology and fossils. What then? What if I made a fool of myself by presuming that he cared about fossils when, in fact, he did not? No, no, that could not be, I decided. He meant what he said, he did care. But he did not come to Lyme at Christmas-time.

In January, I found an enormous crocodile skull in the area of Black Ven. I wanted to tell Henry, but I did not know where he was. I would not dream of asking anyone for his address. Instead, I sent word of my find to Miss Philpot. She came to examine the fossil just as I discovered that I could see the bony plates of the opposite eye though the nostril.

"See," I showed Miss Philpot, "there is no bony separation between the creature's two nostrils."

"There wasn't one in the skull of the first one either, was there?" she remarked.

"No, but we thought it was missing or broken," I said. "But now I can see that the creature did not have one."

"Do all air-breathing creatures have such a bony separation? Do crocodiles?" she asked.

I did not know. We speculated about what the absence of a bony separation between the nostrils might mean and whether the fossil breathed air or water. When she left that afternoon I realized that I had not made any effort to see her or her sisters after I met Henry. I felt ashamed. She and her sisters had been so kind to me, and I had neglected them. I promised myself that never again would I forget my old friends for a new one, no matter who that may be.

Miss Philpot returned a few days later to make me an offer for the crocodile skull. I accepted, and she invited me to come home with her to tea. Mama did not say anything about my going. I think she must have known how lonely I was and was happy to see me out in company. She did not even remark when I described the silver tea service and the china cups so thin you could see the light through them.

A GREAT DISTANCE BETWEEN US

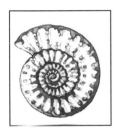 Henry did not return until the spring. It was Joseph who saw him first. He mentioned it to me in passing, and unable to contain myself, I asked in one breath, "Did Mr. de la Beche say anything about stopping by? How long has he been in town? How did he look?"

Joseph sighed and gave me a knowing look. "I did not talk to Mr. de la Beche, Mary. He was deep in conversation with Dr. Carpenter and only nodded in my direction. He looked"—here he chuckled— "he looked quite the young gentleman."

I waited for some word from Henry. I expected a message asking me to meet him on the beach somewhere. I imagined that he might even slip it to me himself, bumping into me as if by chance on the street. I knew it would come. And I knew when he saw me it would be just as it was. Better, perhaps, I thought, remembering that he said that I was the only person he could be himself with, the only person who truly understood him. I imagined him saying, "I have been away and done what my mother wished and, now she understands that I belong here, that I am serious about geology . . . about you." He would look into my eyes when he said this and take my hand in his.

Days passed in which I jumped at every passing footstep. I waited, but no message came.

It was by chance that I saw Henry on Church Cliff beach one day. He was sitting on a rock sketching. He did not see me. I started in his direction, then hesitated. The thought that he might be avoiding me, which I had managed to suppress for so long, seized me with its obviousness. His name died on my lips. At that moment he looked up, and called to me, "Miss Anning, hello." Not Mary, but Miss Anning. Putting the sketchbook aside, he got to his feet and came over to greet me.

"Mr. de la Beche, you are back," I said, welcoming him. "How long have you been here?"

"Ten days," he said. "I was going to stop by the shop, but . . ." and his voice trailed off as he mumbled something about a family wedding. I said all the polite things one says on such occasions. I felt embarrassed, but I did not know how to break the conversation off. He asked me whether I had found any other crocodiles or pieces of the small-headed creature in his absence. I told him that I found an enormous crocodile skull and some ribs and vertebrae. He promised to stop by to see them.

"That would be nice," I replied, unable to think of anything else to say, but still I did not go.

Neither did he. He smiled down at me for what seemed like minutes. His eyes looked sad and uncertain.

A gust of wind riffled the pages of his sketch pad, and we turned in its direction. "I have to get back to work," I said. He nodded and ran off to get his sketch pad before it blew away.

He stopped by the shop a few days later. Although he had only been gone for six months, he seemed different, as Joseph had said, more grown-up, more self-assured, more distant. He examined the bits and pieces of crocodile ribs and vertebrae methodically, while I looked on. He did not speculate as he used to. In fact, he said little. He did say that he would like to draw the pieces of crocodile I had. I suggested that he come the next day. "I could do a better job of it at home," he replied, and I let him take some of it home.

We hunted for fossils over in the clay at Golden Cap. Although it was a long way from town and we were together for hours, there was no running along the beach, no slipping on the pebbles, no dashing between waves, no wild speculations about what we would find. It was serious and businesslike, with many silences and half-finished sentences. I started to point out a bed of belemnites to him and saw by his face that he already knew. We were not successful in the first place we chose to look and were moving on to another site when Henry said, as if he had just happened to think of it, "Did I tell you, I saw our crocodile jaw, the one that was stolen from Black Ven last year? I am certain that it is the same one."

I was surprised by the casualness with which he had dropped this piece of information. "Where did you see it?" I asked. He told me that he went with Dr. Carpenter to visit the collection of a Mr. South who had taken lodgings in Charmouth in order to collect fossils from the Lias. "There it was, displayed along with all of his other fossils just as if it was rightfully his and not stolen. It is the centerpiece of his collection."

"How did Mr. South come to have the jaw?" I asked, wondering if he was the gentlemen that Jim Greengrass had sold it to.

Henry seemed surprised by my question. "I couldn't very well inquire if he did not offer the information. That would not be proper. You do not accuse a gentleman of theft."

"Asking him where he bought it or found it is not an accusation," I retorted.

"But it has that undertone, does it not?" I could see that he was annoyed at me for being insistent. "A gentleman does not need to explain himself, and so I did not ask nor did he offer any information. What does it matter where he bought it? He has it now."

I had to admit that he was right. In one sense, *Henry's* sense, it did not matter how Mr. South came to have the crocodile jaw; it only mattered that it existed and was available for study. For a moment I felt small for caring. But the more I thought about it, the angrier I became. It did matter, for me at least. The bread on our table is purchased with the money I earn from such finds. Only Henry's wealth could make him so removed from the cares and thoughts of others and so blind to my situation.

"It is spectacular," he continued, not noticing that I had fallen silent. "South says it was not a crocodile, but it was some kind of lizard. The joint between the lower jaw and the skull is different from a crocodile's."

How distant we are. I realized that it would never be the same again, not just because of the talk in town. The differences between us are too great to overcome— he is, after all, an educated young man who has a considerable fortune, and I am penniless, a cabinet- maker's daughter. But still I am sad, more than sad, desolate. He is the only other person my age I know who cares about the same things I do. Despite our differences, I admire him, I loved him (though it is painful to write it, even now), and consider him a friend, which I always will. Yet feeling as I do, I have separated myself from others and made myself misera- ble. It is, as I have put down here, all because of the fossils. They have led me into these places, places where I have no business being.

Unfortunately, wishing things had been different does not make them so. A stain on one's reputation is not soon erased. My neighbors and the members of our meeting strongly disapproved of my relations with Henry de la Beche and saw them in the worst possible light. They thought I was being wild and willful in refusing to listen to Mama. They were relieved when Henry went away, thinking that I had narrowly escaped ruin. They hoped that with him no longer there to lead me astray, I would eventually come to my senses.

It is no wonder then that all eyes were on us when Henry and I went out together to Golden Cap that day. Not knowing anything about the change in our relations, our friends and neighbors were certain that we were taking up where we had left off. This time, they decided, if Mama was too weak to stop me, they would. Mrs. Gleed took it upon herself to talk to me.

I was in my shop, working on a fossil the day after our excursion, when the bell on the door rang. I looked up to see Mrs. Gleed entering the shop. I greeted her, telling her that Mama was not in.

"I know that she is not in, and that is why I have come now. I do not wish to upset your poor, dear mama. She already has enough to bear. I wish to speak to you alone, Mary," she said.

I immediately guessed why she had come, and my face reddened with shame and anger. I tried to gain control of my feelings as I got up from the workbench saying, "Please come upstairs, Mrs. Gleed. It would be more comfortable for us to talk in the house."

She refused, saying that she preferred to remain where she was.

I offered her a stool to sit on.

"Trying to be polite now will not deter me, Mary," she said, placing herself at the end of my workbench and staring at me with eyes like daggers. "What I have to say to you can be said standing; I do not wish to spend much time in the company of a girl whose honor is in question."

Though I had expected Mrs. Gleed to scold me, I was not prepared for so direct an attack. "My honor? What, what . . . ?" I stammered.

"Your honor, Mary. Your behavior has given others cause to talk."

"But I have done nothing wrong," I began, in an attempt to defend myself.

She cut me off, "Giving others cause to talk is wrong. Your behavior is unseemly. You have been observed walking on the beach alone with young de la Beche. You have been with him many times. Your mama tried to talk to you, but you would not listen. You tried to hide behind the curiosities. You even had your mama convinced that you were no longer seeing him. But I have it on good authority that you continued to meet him on the beach in secluded places until he went to London."

"We did nothing wrong. We were hunting curiosities," I said. "He pays me for what we find. It is my livelihood."

She sniffed. "Is that what he pays you for, miss?"

"You know that is so!" I cried out. "How could you even suggest otherwise?"

"You dare to ask me how I can say such a thing? Look to your own conduct. It is your behavior that leads me and others to think such things. If you had not given us cause, there would be no such talk. You are being wicked and willful just as I warned your mother you would be if you were not curbed. And your poor mother has not been up to the task of breaking your will. So it falls on others to do it for her," she said with a sigh.

I had disliked Mrs. Gleed since the day she had come to talk to Mama about sending me to the chapel school. Now her self-righteous sigh made me defiant. "Did you talk to Mama? Did Mama ask you to talk to me?" I demanded, the tears running down my cheeks. "Her food is bought with the money de la Beche and others like him pay me."

Mrs. Gleed continued without answering me. "I am speaking on behalf of our meeting and those who care for your mother and the memory of your father. On their behalf I am warning you. You are bringing shame down upon your family. You must no longer see this young gentleman. It is for your own good that I am telling you this, Mary."

My eyes held hers as I struggled to regain my self-control. "You are telling me for my own good what others say. What do they know about hunting curiosities or of making a living doing so? Nothing! They know nothing of what I do, except to talk maliciously about it and about me. It is not fair! They would be happy to see me fail, to see us thrown upon the parish. I tell you that I did nothing wrong in going curiosity hunting with Mr. de la Beche."

"It is not a pleasant task to come here to reason with you, miss," she said, returning my gaze. "I might just as easily let you slide into sin if it were not for your mama and her good name. If you do not want to be shunned by your friends and neighbors you must no longer be seen with him."

"But what of my livelihood? I am paid to take him curiosity hunting. Am I to stop earning a living just because of some idle talk?" I demanded angrily. And then, realizing that my anger would only make things worse, I softened. "We did nothing wrong, I tell you. Nothing!"

"I can see there is no talking to you, miss," she snapped. "You are determined to continue being willful and wicked and will not repent. But do not say that you have not been warned." With that, she turned on her heel, and picking her way through the clutter of the shop with exaggerated care, she opened the door and left.

For a fleeting instant I thought, It isn't fair to punish me so, not now, not after he is lost to me. Perhaps I should have confessed to Mrs. Gleed that things had changed between Henry and me. Our relations were now purely professional. She could be assured that nothing unseemly would ever happen between us. But immediately I rejected the thought, knowing that such a confession would not have helped me. I was glad that I had not stooped so low. Mrs. Gleed would not have believed me no matter what I said. She was determined in her bad opinion of me as long as I went fossil hunting.

It was with some bitterness that I realized that I would never be accepted by our neighbors and belong among them unless I gave up the curiosities altogether. I wish I could give them up. I wish I had never laid eyes on them. I wish Papa had listened to Mama when she objected to my going with him. Then I would be like Lizzie, like the others, and life would be simple and clear.

A DEMEANING FIRST MEETING

Other things happened to make me think that I have taken a wrong turn and am lost in a lonely wilderness from which I must find a way out.

When I was out with Mr. Johnson, who comes from Bristol to Lyme to collect every year, I found a paddle that I thought belonged to the crocodile. If it does indeed belong to the crocodile (which it seems to), it is one more piece of evidence that the fossil differed from modern-day crocodiles, which do not have paddles for swimming, but legs. My find attracted the attention of many people, including the Reverend Buckland, who was in Lyme to collect fossils for Oxford University. I am told that he has started to give lectures there on geology.

The Reverend Buckland stopped by the shop when I was out, leaving a message asking me to send all the pieces of the crocodile I have in my possession to his lodgings early the next morning for examination. I found it an odd and inconvenient request. But since he is a collector and collectors are my best customers, I did my best to comply.

When I arrived at his lodgings on Broad Street, I and

the boy who was helping me were admitted by a girl about my age who, upon seeing the box of fossils, grumbled, "More bones. How am I supposed to keep his room tidy? He hasn't even enough room left to turn around in."

I realized that I was not the first fossilist to visit the Reverend Buckland. I was curious about what the others had brought and whether they had anything as interesting as I had.

She led me up the stairs to a dark hallway with a closed door at the end. "Wait here," she ordered, and turned around and went back downstairs. She came back several minutes later carrying a breakfast tray that she took into the room, still leaving me and the boy standing outside in the dark hallway holding the heavy box of fossils. Through the closed door I heard the tinkle of china as the table was laid. Then there was silence, which was suddenly shattered by a shout, "Idiot! I told you to send her up immediately." The door opened, and the girl stuck her head out into the hall and said, "He wants to see you."

Taking the box of fossils from the boy, I entered a large room with floor-to-ceiling windows at one end. The Reverend Buckland, a big, balding man, was sitting at the breakfast table with a napkin tucked into his shirt front like a bib. He said, "Mary." I nodded my head in his direction, that being the best I could do with the box of fossils in my hands. He did not get up, nor did he introduce himself. He lifted his coffee cup to his lips and eyed me over the rim as he drank. He put his cup down and asked, "Have you brought the paddle along?"

I told him that I no longer had it, Mr. Johnson did. "He was with me when it was found, and he paid me for it," I explained.

"Oh, I see," the Reverend Buckland said, and I could see that he was disappointed. Reaching for a bun, he asked, "Are you the one who collects the fossils?"

"Yes, sir," I replied.

He stopped and peered at me from under his brows. "A young girl like you on the beach and out on those ledges?"

Again I responded affirmatively, and he continued questioning me. He asked how I find fossils and how I extract them from the surrounding rock. He wanted to know whether it is I who clean and develop them or if someone else does it for me. It was evident that he found it surprising that I did these things. As little as a year ago I would have been delighted by his questions and his surprise at finding a female fossilist. Now his surprise made me feel as if I was doing something not only unexpected, but odd and strange—as if I was peculiar.

Having satisfied himself that I actually am a fossilist, he asked if I took people out on fossil-hunting expeditions. I told him that I did, and he said, "Well then, I shall have to go fossil hunting with you soon. It seems that is the only way to obtain the things I wish to collect."

"At your convenience, sir," I replied.

Finally, he noticed the very heavy box I had been struggling with all the while and asked what I brought. When I told him that they were crocodile bones, he corrected me and told me that it was not a crocodile, but some other creature whose nature was being determined by scientists. I knew this, of course, but called the fossil a crocodile for want of a better name. But I did not say anything. I could see that he believed that I did not know anything about the fossils except how to obtain them.

He got up from the table, eager to see what I had. I looked for some place to put the box so that I could take the bones out, but every place I looked was littered with rocks, fossils, books, letters, newspapers, silver tea things, muffins, rolls, butter, jam, papers, bags of dirt, and every other thing imaginable. I could see why the girl complained when she saw my box. The only clear space was a patch of the floor and I bent down and put the box there. The Reverend Buckland was immediately down on his hands and knees beside the box. He examined the bones carefully, especially the vertebrae and ribs, turning them over and over, but saying little, except "By Jove, wait till I write to Home about this," or "What an idiot the man is!" which I could not make

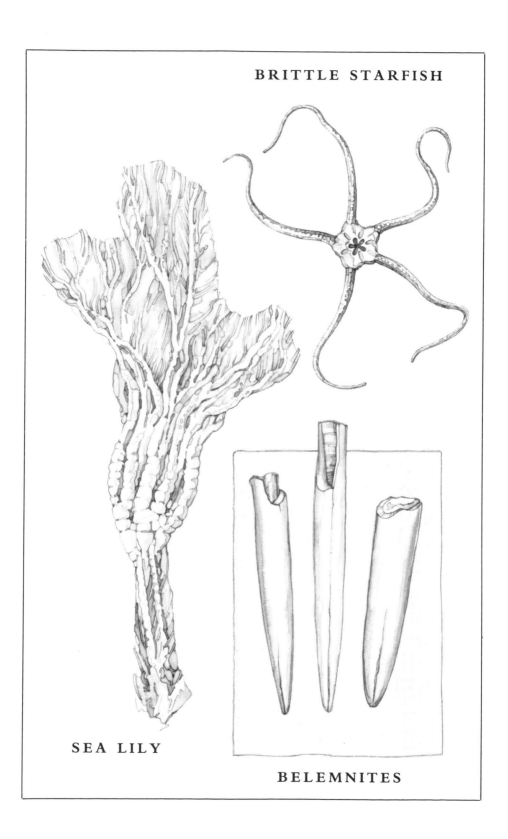

BRITTLE STARFISH

SEA LILY

BELEMNITES

sense of. I did not yet know what he was going to write to Home or even who Home was.

Having made a preliminary examination of the bones, Buckland got to his feet, brushed off his trousers, and asked if he might keep the fossils for a while.

I said, "Yes, of course you may, sir," though he had not made an offer to buy the bones. While he had them I could not sell them to anyone else.

Walking home afterward I regretted allowing the Reverend Buckland to keep the bones. I wished I had let him know that I was not the simple girl he thought I was. I wished I had been able to show him that I knew a thing or two about fossils. In other words, I wished that I had not been as silent, submissive, and subservient as I had been. Not because I wanted him to think better of me. I know people like him do not have it in them to give people of the lower classes their due. We are all little more than beasts placed on earth to serve the likes of him, or so they often seem to think. No, it is not that I wanted him to think better of me, but that I did not want him to make me feel as if I am what he thinks I am and nothing more. I am not just a hunting guide, a pointer who discovers fossils, instead of pheasants.

OTHERS GET THE CREDIT

 A few days after my call on the Reverend Buckland, Miss Philpot dropped by the shop with the news that there was a description of the crocodile in the *Philosophical Transactions of the Royal Society* by a Sir Everard Home. "I have only just heard about it from Dr. Carpenter, who says that Buckland told him about it," she told me excitedly. "He says that Buckland told him that Sir Home is a comparative anatomist, just the kind of man we have been hoping would get his hands on the fossil. Now we can find out for certain what kind of animal it was."

Pulling out a stool and sitting down at the workbench, Miss Philpot continued, "Dr. Carpenter told me that Buckland has a copy of the paper, which he promised to lend him as soon as he is finished with it. Dr. Carpenter said that as soon as he has read it and passed it around among the other geological gentlemen of Lyme, he plans to have a little party so that they can discuss what this Sir Home wrote."

"Please tell me what they say, Miss Philpot," I said. "I am most eager to know everything."

"I would, dear, but I cannot. I have not been invited;

it will only be gentlemen, so we shall both have to depend on Dr. Carpenter's report."

I was about to protest that she knew more about the crocodile than the other gentlemen, but before I could, she explained, "Dr. Carpenter says that if he invited the ladies it would change the nature of the discussion because they do not understand science, with the exception of me, of course. But, I can well see that he cannot invite me and no other ladies, so it will be gentlemen only."

"And you are to be excluded," I remarked, thinking it natural that I be excluded from such company.

"Yes, yes," she said with a smile. "But, Mary, my dear, I do not intend to remain ignorant, I promise you that. I will obtain a copy of the *Philosophical Transactions of the Royal Society,* and when I do you shall see it."

Miss Philpot was as good as her word. A week or so later she stopped by the shop with the volume in hand. "How did you manage to get your hands on it?" I asked, eyeing it hungrily.

She laughed. "Simple, everything is simple when you have something others want. The Reverend Buckland has heard that I have interesting fossils in my cabinet. He was eager to see them. I told Dr. Carpenter to tell Buckland that he could come and spend as long as he liked examining my collection if I could borrow his copy of the *Transactions.* He came with the copy. I must say I think that the Reverend Buckland got the better part of the deal. I am somewhat disappointed. This Home fellow . . ." She sighed. "I do not know what to say. I think it's better for you to read and form your own opinion."

I began reading *"Some account of the fossil remains of an animal more nearly allied to Fishes than any of the other classes of animals"* as soon as the door closed behind Miss Philpot. I turned first to look at the beautifully done engravings of the fossil. After examining them carefully I turned to the text, which begins with the statement,

"The study of comparative anatomy is not confined to the animals that at present inhabit the earth, but extends to the remains of such as existed in the most remote periods of antiquity; among these may be classed the specimen which forms the subject of the present Paper."

It seems that this Sir Home believes that the crocodile, as we have been calling it, is extinct. He states this simply as if it is evident to all reasonable people.

Home continues, stating that comparative anatomy

"not only brings to our knowledge races of animals very different from those with which we are acquainted, but supplies intermediate links in the gradation of structure, by means of which the different classes will probably be found so imperceptibly to run into one another, that they will no longer be accounted distinct, but only portions of one series,

*and show that the whole of the animal creation forms a
regular and connected chain."*

I wonder whether he means that the fossil crocodile is
different from anything we know now, and is, perhaps,
somewhere in between fishes and lizards, a link between
the two? He also seems to be saying that it is possible
that when we discover other intermediate links like the
fossil crocodile, we will see that instead of distinct
classes of animals that are separate from one another in
structure as there is now, there was once a regular,
connected chain of animal life in which the structure of
one class of animals subtly shaded into the next.

From this Home goes on to praise Bullock, in whose
museum of natural history the fossil is displayed, for
removing the surrounding stone. I cannot understand
why Sir Home praises Bullock when it is I who have
removed the stone so that the parts of the fossil can be
seen. He also describes the situation in which the fossil
was found, mentioning Squire Henley on whose estate
it was entombed. I look in vain for my name or for
some mention of the fossil being found by a girl, but
there is none. It is as if I never hunted for the fossil,
found it, dug it out, or prepared it; as if I was not part
of it. As if I did not exist!

I was deeply hurt, but I continued reading. Sir Home
wrote that the bones in which the nostril is situated are
broken, although I know they are not. The nostrils are

the same in the skull I most recently found. There is no bony separation between them. He says that such nostrils correspond to those in fishes, but I disagree. They seem more like those in birds. He concludes that while the jaws, which extend backward beyond the skull, are more like those of the crocodile than like any fishes that are presently known, in other particulars such as the way in which the lower jaw is connected to the skull, the way in which the ribs are connected to the vertebrae, and the bony coat of the eye the fossil resembles a fish.

I pushed Home's account aside. It may not have been a crocodile, but it certainly was not a fish! Even I know that, and I am no comparative anatomist. He does not know what it is, except to say that it has features of both. We had been waiting for this account for so long, and it turned out to be so disappointing and inconclusive.

Miss Philpot asked me what I thought of Sir Home's description when I returned the *Transactions* to her. I said little, afraid of sounding bitter.

"I can see that you do not think much of it," she said with a laugh. "Now you shall have to find another specimen so that he has more evidence and can fill in the blanks and correct his errors."

"I don't care to," I said. "What does it matter if I do find another, or if I disagree with him and think he has things wrong? He would not listen to me. He does not even know that I exist. Nor do the others, and they do not care because I do not matter to them." I wanted to say I hate the whole lot of them, but I didn't.

"Buckland is aware of your existence, that is for certain. He told me that he has some ribs and vertebrae from you and that he was most impressed with them and with you. If you point out what you think Home's errors are to him, perhaps he will write to Home and inform him," she said.

I nodded as if I agreed, but said nothing. Of course Buckland would write to Home. And he would get the credit for it. Why should I tell him? Why should I tell anyone? I want to get credit for what I do. Why shouldn't I? Because I am a female? Because I am a person who earns her bread by her own labor? I did the work, and I do not want to be robbed of my due by "geological gentlemen" or by anyone else.

Why am I in this business? I must be mad to continue. I am scorned by the townspeople and by our friends and neighbors who do not understand me or sympathize with me. They think I am strange to do such work, an oddity, not quite respectable. And the gentry, the "geological gentry," agrees. I shall not forget that interview with the Reverend Buckland, his surprise at finding that it was I who found the fossils and dug them out, his certainty that I am little more than a dumb beast who sniffs out fossils but does not care or know what they are. Nor will I forget my interview with Lizzie that day in the shop or the more recent scolding from Mrs.

Gleed. I shall not forget Robert Cruikshanks's glee when the fossil I found was stolen, either. No, I shan't forget.

Henry de la Beche is the only one who understands my work, but he does not understand that it is my livelihood, nor does he care for me. I must be mad. Why can't I just give it up and be like others?

I slept little that night. I tossed and turned and woke exhausted. At breakfast Mama said something about my looking poorly. I confessed that I was not feeling well, but I did not tell her it was because I had been made to feel small, insignificant, an oddity by the very gentlemen who buy my fossils. That would be unthinkable. That was precisely what she was afraid of. Did she not warn Papa when he wanted to take me out fossil hunting that it was not a proper pursuit for girls? Did she not warn me that I had no place with the gentry? Yet she is always glad enough for the money I earn selling fossils to the gentry, isn't she? My porridge grew cold in the bowl in front of me.

I could do nothing right in the shop. I started to work on a fossil and put it down. I found that I had spent the morning staring into space. Tears were rolling down my cheeks, and I made no effort to wipe them away. I was not crying in sorrow, but in anger, anger at my life, at everyone—at Lizzie Adams, at Caroline Gleed, Jane Lovell, Adam Garrison, William Trowbridge, Robert Cruikshanks, Mrs. Harris the schoolteacher, at Mrs.

Gleed, at the housekeeper at High Cliffs, and all the rest
of them who have made my life a misery, for their lack
of understanding, their mean-spirited gossip, their cru-
elty, their hurts. I was angry at Henry de la Beche for
being a coward, for being so much "the young gentleman" he is, for not being what I wanted him so much
to be. I was angry at Squire Henley for taking advantage
of me by paying me little when he has so much; at Mr.
South for not caring how he comes by his fossils; at Sir
Everard Home, at everyone. It was a long list of pain
that I was recalling, and I was breathing as hard with
the exertion of remembering as if I had scaled a cliff.

The bell on the door rang and a well-dressed man
entered the shop. I wiped away my tears with my sleeve.
He picked through the fossils on the shelves. "Are you
looking for anything in particular?" I asked, coming to
help him from the workbench. He did not say anything,
but continued. "I see you are determined to amuse
yourself by making work for me," I said. The man
colored. "You do not have what I am looking for," he
mumbled, and retreated. Immediately I was sorry that
I had driven him away. The man had done nothing
wrong, and I attacked him and lost his trade. My head
hurt, and I felt hot.

I told Mama I was going out and asked her to mind
the shop. I walked. I walked without purpose or destination, oblivious to all I passed. I walked out of town
and along the undercliffs until I was exhausted from

walking and turned back toward home. As I was cross-
ing Coombe Street someone shouted, and I looked up
just in time to see a carriage drawn by a pair of horses
racing toward me. I was dashed against the wall in my
efforts to escape. My cheek was scraped and bleeding,
and I was stunned with pain. Onlookers scolded me for
not watching where I was going, telling me that I might
have been killed. I nodded, agreeing with them, and
walked away.

When I returned, Mama was still in the workshop
where I left her. My strange behavior had made her
anxious, and she was alarmed by the sight of my cheek.
But when she asked what was the matter, I only nodded
wearily and told her that it was a little scrape that I
would wash off. She followed me to the scullery and
watched as I poured some water on a towel and wiped
my face.

"You are not well," she remarked. "Perhaps you had
better lie down." I only nodded and started up the stairs.
She locked the door to the shop and followed me up.
She watched anxiously as I took off my shoes, stockings,
and dress. She did not know what to think. I have never
gone to bed in the middle of the day before. When I
was lying down, she covered me. She sat on the end of
the bed for a while before going back to her work.

I fell into a dream-filled sleep. I dreamt that I was in
the marketplace with my basket. It is filled with fossils.
Gentlemen in top hats come by and help themselves to

the fossils, without saying a word to me. Soon I have no more fossils, but they continue to come and come until the marketplace is filled with men in black coats and top hats. They take away my clothes. When I have no clothes, they cut at my hair. Soon they are pounding at my arms and legs with geological hammers. Someone has taken a chisel and hammer to my head. I plead with them to stop, but they do not seem to be able to hear me. I cry, but still they continue. With great effort I stand up, throwing them off. Surprised, the gentlemen step away from me. They proceed to point at me and talk among themselves about me. "Go away! Leave me alone! I am a person, not a curiosity," I yell. They laugh and run away, leaving me alone in the deserted marketplace.

I dreamt that I was talking to the Reverend Buckland about Home's paper. I have something very important to tell him, and he is eager to hear what I have to say. I open my mouth to speak, but no sound comes out, I am mute.

I stayed in bed for the remainder of that day. That night and all of the next day I thought over what happened. I could not go on as I had been, scorned by all, with no one who understood me. I kept telling myself that I must find something else to do. It was madness to keep on working at something that caused me such pain. I could learn to make lace like Mama, she would be glad to teach me. She had been teaching

Ann—poor, dear Ann. I could learn another trade, any other trade. But each time I thought of some other pursuit, I found fault with it. I was confused and lost.

It was dark outside. The day had passed. Across the room I could hear Mama's even breathing. I grabbed a shawl and threw it round my shoulders. I stole down the stairs barefoot. I lit a candle from the coals in the fireplace, opened the door, and went to my workshop. There I took out this daybook given to me for my fifteenth birthday by Joseph and began this account.

A GEOLOGICAL TEA PARTY

 I have been stealing down to the shop at night to write for several weeks now. At last, I believe I have reached my destination—the present. All that remains is for me to include here a description of the event that brought me out of my despair and helped me to see my life more clearly.

Miss Philpot had a tea party to which everyone in the district who took an interest in geology was invited, including Mr. de la Beche and me, Miss Mary Anning. At first, I was doubtful about accepting the invitation. I felt that I did not belong at such an affair. I am younger than everyone else invited, except for Henry, by at least ten years. I was certain that I would be uncomfortable at such a gathering. And yet I wanted to go. Aside from Miss Mary Philpot, Miss Elizabeth's older sister, everyone who was to be there was interested in fossils. All of them had bought fossils from me and talked with me about them. And despite everything, my isolation, the slurs and insults, I very much wanted to hear what was said.

Caught between my desire to go, and the certainty that I should not, I did not respond to Miss Philpot's invitation. The next day Miss Philpot stopped by the shop to see if I was ill. She found me looking well, working at my usual place. She tried to ferret out my reason for not responding to her invitation. We chatted for a few minutes, but I did not explain myself. As she was leaving, she said, "I will be very disappointed if you do not come to tea, Mary. I am counting on you to help my sister Margaret and me show these men that the female sex is capable of understanding science and that we are not the empty-headed, foolish creatures they take us to be."

I did not tell her that I thought that she would fail, that all such attempts are doomed from the start. How could I, when she is so cheerfully persistent and such a good friend to me? I realized that I had to go because she believed that I could make a difference, even if I did not believe it.

On the appointed day I put on my best gown, which has a blue-flowered pattern on a white ground, new shoes with stand-up heels, new stockings, a blue tippet with frills all round, and my bonnet with the sky blue underside and blue ribbons. I started out for the Philpots' house on Silver Street at about four o'clock and made my way up Broad Street with a mixture of dread and anticipation. The invitation was for four-thirty and Lyme being such a small place, I was early. I was admitted by Betty, who told me that the Philpot sisters were still dressing and would be down shortly. She led me into the empty drawing room. Through the door I could see the tea table laden with ham, pickles, cheese, cakes, cream, sweetmeats, and the good Lord only knows what else.

I waited, growing more anxious with every passing moment. Miss Mary entered first and came over to welcome me. She was wearing a sheer white muslin gown with many tucks. Next to her elegance, my printed cotton gown seemed simple and poor. I wished I had not come, but it was too late to leave. Dr. Carpenter, the Reverend Buckland, and Henry de la Beche all arrived at once, followed by Mr. Johnson and Mr. South. If any of the gentlemen were surprised to find themselves in my company, they did not show it, but greeted me cordially, calling me Miss Anning.

Almost at once, they entered into a heated conversation about how the earth had been shaped. I was ignorant of the theories that they were discussing and sat quietly, listening. I was acutely aware that Henry was standing only a few feet away. He, for his part, seemed to be oblivious to my presence as he talked with Mr. South about the different strata of the cliffs in our neighborhood. How sure of himself he seems, I thought, feeling miserable. He belongs here, but I do not. I should never have come. It was a mistake.

The conversation died down, and we went in to tea. I found that I was seated at the far end of the room from Henry, beside the Reverend Buckland. He turned toward me so that we were facing one another. "We have all been talking about your fossil, Miss Anning," he said, making polite conversation with me. "It must have been quite an extraordinary thing to discover something like that. A shock, I would think. What did you think when you first saw it?"

I was determined to say little, but he smiled at me in such an encouraging, warm way that I found myself telling him that I did not see the entire thing all at once, only the eye and a few teeth, ". . . but when I saw it I knew that I had found what people called the crocodile, sir. As it turned out, it was only the head. It took almost a year before I found the body."

The Reverend Buckland helped himself to a large piece of ham from the platter that was being passed around by Betty. "People had been talking about a crocodile, then?" he asked.

"We had been finding very large fossil vertebrae for some time," I continued, forgetting myself as I took food from the platter. "People said that they belonged to a crocodile or a dragon. At least that is what my father told me when I found a vertebrae the first time I went out curiosity hunting with him. He said there was talk of a large creature buried in the cliffs."

"Since you are not very old now, you must have been quite young at the time," the Reverend Buckland said, encouraging me to continue.

"I am fifteen years old, sir," I responded, glowing

with pride. "I have been hunting fossils since I was seven. I first went out with my father." The Reverend Buckland shook his head sympathetically and smiled at me, making me wonder how I could ever have disliked him or been angry at him, though he still had not paid for the fossils I had left with him.

At this point Mr. South, who was seated on my other side, joined in the conversation, telling the Reverend Buckland that it was he who first introduced my father to fossil hunting. "You know that Mr. Anning was a cabinetmaker, but in a small town like Lyme there isn't much call for the fine work he did, and he had to find some means of adding to his income. He was quick to learn and good at finding fossils and preparing them. An honest fellow."

Complimentary though it was, I was discomforted by Mr. South's description of Papa in this setting. But before I could change the topic, Miss Elizabeth, who had overheard Mr. South, added, "Many of us here can testify to Mr. Anning's fine craftsmanship. But I believe that his finest accomplishment is his daughter, Mary, whom he trained. Without her keen eye and her careful workmanship we would not all be here discussing the crocodile today."

Hearing the word "crocodile," I seized the opportunity to turn the conversation away from personal matters and asked the Reverend Buckland whether it was known when the crocodile lived. It was something that

I had been wondering about ever since I became aware of its existence.

At this question, the Reverend Buckland put down his knife and fork, straightened and turned to address the room. "As you know from Sir Home's paper, it was not a crocodile, but an animal allied with the fishes," he said, his voice no longer intimate and soft, but loud and authoritative. "No doubt it lived before the flood. Lyme's cliffs were under the sea then and that is why you find fossils of creatures that lived in the sea entombed in the cliffs. When God pulled back the waters after the deluge, the cliffs became part of the land."

"Sir, are you speaking of Noah's Flood?" Miss Mary asked.

"It is unlikely to have been Noah's Flood," I interjected, not thinking about the effect such a comment might have on Miss Mary.

"Why do you say that?" Miss Mary demanded, turning to face me angrily.

Seeing how upset she was, I was immediately sorry that I had said anything, and though all eyes were on me, waiting for my reply, I could not think of what to say next.

Henry, whose eyes had been avoiding mine up until that moment, now looked directly at me across the expanse of the room and smiled in a way that seemed to say, we've talked about this before, Mary, haven't we? "It stands to reason that if it was Noah's Flood that covered the cliffs, there should be some signs of human existence left behind," he said, as everyone turned from me to him. "But Miss Anning has never seen any traces of man or fossilized human bones mixed in with the creatures she finds in the cliffs. That is why she says it is unlikely that it was Noah's Flood."

Finished with his explanation, he glanced to see what my response was. I gave him an approving smile. It had been a difficult moment for me and he had understood.

After Henry's explanation, the Reverend Buckland moved forward in his chair, recapturing the attention of the group. "It seems that there was a deluge as described in the Holy Scriptures, Miss Philpot, but Mr. de la Beche and Miss Anning are correct that there is some doubt that it was the very same one. The earth has gone through several changes during its long history, and God has created new forms of life suitable for the new conditions on earth each time."

Miss Mary Philpot put her teacup down on the table with a clatter, interrupting the Reverend Buckland. He stopped and looked to her as did the rest of us. There were scarlet patches on her cheeks, and her voice was high with tension, "Sir, need I remind you that the Holy Bible speaks of only one creation and that one was accomplished in six days."

"Now, Mary," Miss Elizabeth said soothingly, "you

know that it doesn't do to mix up geology with the Holy Scriptures. We must not be too literal in our reading of the Scriptures."

"Your sister is correct, Miss Philpot," the Reverend Buckland added. "The Holy Bible was not written to teach scientific truth, but to reveal God to us and to instruct us in divine life. It took a long time to create the world we live in, an unimaginable length of time. Perhaps the beginning that is spoken of in the Scriptures is all the time before the creation of man. The facts of geology do not dispute the Scriptures. In fact they show us everywhere the benevolence of our Creator."

Mary Philpot shook her head in disagreement and whispered something into her sister Margaret's ear, something disapproving evidently, because she soon got up and with much fluttering left the room.

But I did not disapprove. I was excited by what the Reverend Buckland was saying, exhilarated to find that I am not the only one who has seen these things and not the only one to have such questions. The Reverend Buckland is a respected, learned gentleman, a man of God, and yet he is troubled by the same questions that trouble me.

I cannot give up hunting fossils, not now. I want to find fossils for him and for those like him, who are trying to read the record of the world's history. I want to be numbered among those who are working to un-cover the mystery of the earth and life on it, even if my part is a small one. It is a noble endeavor, and I must be part of it. Of course, I did not say anything about this to him or to anyone else. It is a private resolve.

After tea was served, we all trooped back into the drawing room to continue our talk. I was anxious as I saw Henry approach me, not quite knowing what I would say, but he soon put me at my ease. "Did I give a fair representation of your position, Miss Anning?" he asked. The question was straightforward, but his eyes were laughing.

Perhaps he would never be the kind of companion I had wished he would be, but I realized that he was still my friend, a geological friend. And I am grateful to have such a friend. I nodded. "Yes. Thank you," I said. "I certainly got myself into a pickle with Miss Mary, didn't I?"

He smiled at me. "It is an easy enough pickle to get into with people who don't understand anything about geology or science. I know I've been in a few myself."

"Do you think it will ever change?" I asked.

His expression became earnest. "That people will be less ignorant and benighted? I don't know. But I have hope that as we continue to find evidence and to inform the public about our discoveries, science will prevail."

"I do, too," I said.

At that moment the Reverend Buckland broke into our conversation, saying, "I am determined to write to Home about the ribs and vertebrae you so kindly allowed me to study. The man needs to be set straight. He wrote in the *Transactions* that the mode of attachment of the ribs in the fossil animal is like those found in fishes, but he is wrong."

"You might also write Home that there was no bony separation between the nostrils in the skull that Miss Anning found recently," added Miss Elizabeth, who had just moved her chair to sit nearby.

"I think Home wrote that it was broken or missing," Mr. South said, challenging her. I held my breath awaiting Miss Elizabeth's response.

"Yes, I think he did," Miss Elizabeth replied mildly. "It was an easy error to fall into with only one example. But I have discussed the matter with Miss Anning, and now that there are two such heads available for study and neither shows any evidence of such a bony separation it seems entirely possible that the creature did not have one. I've looked into the matter and found that birds do not have such a separation between their nostrils. That seems significant to me."

"Are you suggesting then, Miss Philpot, that the creature was related to the birds?" Mr. South asked sharply.

"I am suggesting no such thing, sir," Miss Elizabeth replied, standing her ground. "Only that not all animals have such a bony separation. And that among those that do not, are the birds, which breathe air."

Mr. South retreated from this battle into silence. I was pleased that Miss Elizabeth had not withered under his sharp attack and had held her ground, showing him that she was able to participate in real scientific debate. And I was touched that she had acknowleged me.

Mr. Johnson, who had been listening to all of this with interest, said that he also intended to write to Home to inform him of the newly found paddle that he had bought from me. He thinks Home is mistaken in believing the animal to be allied to fishes. It is, he believes, related to lizards, an extinct group of lizards that possessed paddles for swimming.

There was much discussion in the room about this proposal, which ended when Mr. Johnson said, "With all of us contributing evidence as it is found, the truth of the matter will soon be determined."

"But someone must find the evidence first, and that is where you come in, Miss Anning," the Reverend Buckland said to me with a gallant nod in my direction. "Your talents at uncovering the evidence are crucial to this enterprise."

A compliment is a small thing, yet it is this remark that decided me. Some might call it vanity, but it is not the Reverend Buckland's flattery that has turned me around. It is the recognition that I really do have a role to play in the discovery. I had seen immediately that Henry was at home in such discussions as we had had at that tea party, but I had been mistaken in believing that I did not have a place there, too. Now I can see that I do. I cannot stop hunting fossils now while we are still trying to learn what it is I found in the cliffs. I know what I must do.

AN UNDERSTANDING

Reading over this account of my life, I can see that, from the beginning, my fate has been guided by fossils. They have been the center of my existence since the first time I went fossil hunting with Papa and Joseph, and even before. At first it might have been because Joseph was doing it that I wanted to hunt fossils, but soon enough it was the fossils themselves and the thrill of the hunt that held me. But even more than the fossils themselves, it was my fascination with their mystery that made me continue. And it has been this fascination that has sustained me through losses and hardships. It has even led to triumphs, small though they be. If ever Papa gave me anything it was this.

Mama maintained from the beginning that allowing me to go down to the beach to hunt fossils would make people talk, but that did not keep me from wanting to go. The name-calling and taunting at school did not cool my passion for the beach and the cliffs; nor did the hardships of earning our bread in this way. It was too late for me to turn back, even then when I was only a seven-year-old starting school. I was already captive to the strange stones, clues to unimaginable worlds that preceded our own. And in being so captivated I was made different from others; I could not fit in, would not fit in. I did work that my neighbors and friends thought strange for a girl; work that many did not approve of. And this work led me to wonder about things that they do not wonder about and to think thoughts that they do not think.

My work has brought me in contact with people from other classes who are as captivated as I am by fossils and the story they tell of a world prior to our own, but I have found that I do not belong among them either. The fossils are my livelihood, not just something to collect and study.

It is somewhere in between the two—the Lyme of my neighbors and the world of the geological gentry— that I must find a place for myself. It is not a place where others have stood before. But I will find it, and standing there, I will make room for others to stand, too.

EPILOGUE

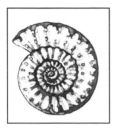 Although there were other occasions when she despaired of her profession and spoke of finding some other occupation, Mary Anning continued hunting fossils to the end of her life.

In 1816, Sir Everard Home published another paper in the *Transactions of the Philosophical Society* based on the paddle, the ribs, and the vertebrae that Mary Anning had found and sold to Mr. Johnson and the Reverend Buckland. As in the first account, Sir Home named the owners of the fossils and thanked them for their communications. Mary Anning is not mentioned. This pattern was repeated in the accounts that Sir Home published in the *Philosophical Transactions of the Royal Society* in 1818 and 1819.

The discovery of posterior paddles showed that the fossil could not be any kind of fish, as Sir Home had first supposed it to be, but was an animal intermediate between a fish and a lizard. The only animal that he could find that was not a fish yet had similar vertebrae was the salamander, Proteus, and thus he named the fossil animal Proteosaurus in a paper he read in 1819. Charles Konig proposed that the animal be called ichthyosaur, or "fish lizard," which is what it is called today.

Since that time it has been discovered that it bore its young live, had skin, not scales, and in many ways resembled a dolphin. It lived 180 million years ago.

In 1824, almost ten years after she found the first "small-headed" creature's bones, Mary Anning found the first complete skeleton of the plesiosaur, a long-necked creature that looked somewhat like a snake threaded through a turtle that lived alongside the ichthyosaur in the sea. She sold the fossil to the Duke of Buckingham for 150 guineas. He bought it on behalf of members of the Geological Society of London.

In 1828 she discovered the first British specimen of a pterosaur, or "winged lizard," the gliding lizardlike creature that lived 160 to 180 million years ago. One or two fragments had been found before, but Mary Anning's specimen was nearly complete and allowed the Reverend Buckland to describe and name the creature. Mary Anning also discovered many small fossil marine creatures.

Though several scientists of the time used Mary Anning's finds to establish their own scientific reputations, she never received the recognition that she should have had. Species are usually named by the person who first describes them in the scientific literature. No one thought to name any of the creatures Mary Anning discovered in her honor. Instead, they were named for the people who bought them from her or for those who first described them in print. Even her discovery of the ichthyosaur was contested. After her death, her nephew, Charles Churchill Anning, wrote to Henry de la Beche that it was not Mary, but her brother Joseph who first discovered the ichthyosaur head in 1812. It is impossible to determine whether Charles Churchill Anning's assertion is true or whether it was an attempt to take credit away from Mary Anning when she was no longer able to defend herself. In any event, it was Mary Anning, and not Joseph, who was the fossilist.

Henry de la Beche's interest in geology was not a passing fancy. At the age of twenty-one, he became a member of the Geological Society of London, at that time the most important forum for discussions of geology and paleontology and for the presentation of new findings in Great Britain. He wrote many scientific papers and was the author of a popular text on geology. He founded the Geological Survey of Great Britain and was its first director. He remained on friendly terms with Mary Anning throughout her life.

When she died at the age of forty-seven, de la Beche, who was then President of the Geological Society, granted her the unique honor of reading the following obituary in the Society's annual notices. It is the only obituary ever accorded a non-member of the society.

*   *   *

I cannot close this notice of our losses by death without adverting to that of one, who though not placed among even the easier classes of society, but who had to earn her daily bread by her labor, yet contributed by her talents and untiring researches in no small degree to our knowledge of the great Enaliosaurians, and other forms of organic life entombed in the vicinity of Lyme Regis. Mary Anning was the daughter of Richard Anning, a cabinetmaker of that town, and was born in May, 1799.

. . . From her father, who appears to have been the first to collect and sell fossils in that neighborhood, she learnt to search for and obtain them. Her future life was dedicated to this pursuit by which she gained her livelihood; and there are those among us in this room who know well how to appreciate the skill she employed (from her knowledge of the various works as they appeared on the subject), in developing the remains of the many fine skeletons of Ichthyosauri and Plesiosauri, which without her care would never have been presented to comparative anatomists in the uninjured form so desirable for their examination. The talents and good conduct of Mary Anning made her many friends; she received a small sum of money for her services, at the intercession of a member of this Society with Lord Melborne when that nobleman was premier. This, with some additional aid, was expended upon an annuity, and

with it, the kind assistance of friends at Lyme Regis, and some little aid derived from the sale of fossils, when her health permitted, she bore with fortitude the progress of a cancer on her breast, until she finally sunk beneath its ravages on the 9th of March, 1847.

ABOUT THE AUTHOR

 Because there are so few known facts about Mary Anning, Sheila Cole decided that the truest way to tell her story was through fiction. She spent years researching the story, including living in England for a year. She walked along the beaches in Lyme Regis where Mary worked and read her day book in The British Museum in London. Even more than the scientific work, it was Mary Anning's character that intrigued Ms. Cole and inspired her to write.

Ms. Cole has written for both children and adults and has had articles published in many national magazines. Her most recent book for Lothrop is *When the Tide Is Low*. Married and the mother of two children, she lives in Solana Beach, CA.